Captain Stanfield halted in the doorway. For a moment he thought he must have taken a wrong turn, for he did not recognize the fashionable young lady who sat with her back to the door.

"Pardon me," he said, coming forward. "Are you lost? May I be of assistance?"

It was only when she turned around and he noticed her spectacles that William realized he was looking at Ariel. He must have said her name aloud, and with some astonishment, for she answered with some asperity.

"You needn't say it as though you find my appearance so incredible or ridiculous."

He moved forward a trifle more quickly than usual and found himself a chair to draw up next to hers.

"I think you look wonderful," William said. "I was taken by surprise, only because I had not seen the lovely young woman behind the bun fastened at the back of your neck, the ink-stained fingers, the spectacles, and the old-fashioned dresses you wore. And my fingers itch to remove your spectacles and undo the bun, perhaps even to gather your hair up into a topknot, so that the curls would fall about your face."

# Miss Tibbles
# Interferes

## April Kihlstrom

A SIGNET BOOK

SIGNET
Published by New American Library, a division of
Penguin Putnam Inc., 375 Hudson Street,
New York, New York 10014, U.S.A.
Penguin Books Ltd, 80 Strand,
London WC2R 0RL, England
Penguin Books Australia Ltd, Ringwood,
Victoria, Australia
Penguin Books Canada Ltd, 10 Alcorn Avenue,
Toronto, Ontario, Canada M4V 3B2
Penguin Books (N.Z.) Ltd, 182–190 Wairau Road,
Auckland 10, New Zealand

Penguin Books Ltd, Registered Offices:
Harmondsworth, Middlesex, England

First published by Signet, an imprint of New American Library,
a division of Penguin Putnam Inc.

First Printing, June 2002
10  9  8  7  6  5  4  3  2  1

This book is dedicated to the memory of my father-in-law, Israel Gerver. I will always be grateful that he was part of my life. Among the things I am grateful for is the depth and breadth of his intellectual interests. It was in the personal and professional library he left behind that I found much of the information I needed for this book.

# 1

Ariel Hawthorne stared at her father. "All of this?" she asked bewildered. "How are you going to organize all of this on your own, Papa?"

The Honorable Mr. Richard Hawthorne waved a hand in the general direction of the unexpected largess. "Oh, I shall manage. It must be done, you know. The trustees are talking about building a new building, one with far more room, and they will expect everything to be cataloged by then. And you know that everyone else is busy with other responsibilities. No, no, we must do this ourselves."

Ariel sighed and settled her spectacles more firmly on her nose. She loved her father; she really did. But he was the most impractical figure imaginable, a circumstance her mother had lamented until the day she died and consigned her husband to her daughter's care. Ariel tried again.

"Why don't you ask some of the soldiers who served in the war to help you catalog what is here?"

He paused and looked at her, then slowly smiled. "What a splendid notion. You are brilliant, Ariel, absolutely brilliant! That is precisely what I shall do! I shall go and write to my old friend Merriweather. We were friends at school together. He was a colonel in the Peninsula, you know. He will know what all these things are and where they came from. He may even have been present when some of them were collected!"

As her father hurried away to his office at the museum, Ariel stared at the piles of objects that had been brought here. Spoils of war, she thought, and not happily. She despised war. And however necessary it might sometimes be, she could not like the notion of celebrating something that had caused so much sorrow and death.

So intent was she on her thoughts that Ariel was completely unaware of the presence of any other person in the hall until that person cleared his throat.

Startled, Ariel turned to see a young man, one arm in a sling, leaning on a cane and staring at her. She took a step toward him, for he looked so pale that she feared he might collapse at any moment.

"I am very sorry, sir," she said, "but this part of the museum is not open to visitors just yet. You must have gotten lost. If you will sit for a moment, I shall find someone who can take you back to the main hall."

He waved her away. "I am not here to view the exhibits. My name is Stanfield, Captain William Stanfield, and I was sent here to help with the artifacts his lordship, Wellington I mean, has presented to the museum." He hesitated, then added, "I served with him in the Peninsula."

"Yes, but you ought to sit," Ariel insisted. She grabbed the nearest straight-back chair and started toward him with it. "You look dreadfully pale. Are you certain that you are well enough to be here?"

"Yes, of course I am," he said.

Captain Stanfield seemed to draw himself to his full height, and Ariel could not help but wish to smooth down his unruly dark blond curls or straighten the jacket that was slightly disarranged by the sling that cradled his arm. A sling, she realized with some surprise and amusement, that had been embroidered with lots of tiny flowers. But he was not smiling, and Ariel found herself wanting to ease the pain she thought she saw in his blue eyes, despite his claims to the contrary.

"I am here, and I shall do as I have been asked to do," Captain Stanfield told her in an austere voice. "If you will find Mr. Hawthorne and tell him I am here, I should be grateful, Miss—?"

"Miss Hawthorne," she said with a smile. "And I shall go fetch my father straightaway, but only if you promise to sit in this chair until I return. I will not have you collapsing on me, as my father has done upon occasion!"

For a moment he hesitated, then bowed slightly. "As you wish," he said. "I should much dislike to be the cause of worry or distress for you."

And with that parting shot, he sat on the chair she had pushed toward him. Ariel blinked, then turned on her heel and marched down the hall to her father's office. She could not imagine what there was about the fellow that should overset her in such a way. She was, after all, accustomed to dealing with all sorts of men; so why should one injured soldier set her pulse racing in such a tumultuous way? And why on earth, she wondered, did he have flowers embroidered on his sling?

Captain William Stanfield stared after Miss Hawthorne. He had not expected or wanted to find a woman here at the British Museum. Granted, she seemed a sensible sort. She wore serviceable clothing and spectacles, and her blond hair had been drawn back into an unfashionable but practical knot at the base of her neck. Clearly she was here to work.

Stanfield sighed. He ought to be thinking about his assignment, not Hawthorne's daughter. She was an unexpected complication, but surely one he could ignore. It was just, he thought, that there was a kindness and a quiet competence about her that he found attractive. He had been alone—and happy that way—for so long that he found the sensation rather disconcerting.

At that moment, the young woman returned with her father. Mr. Hawthorne was positively rubbing his hands together with glee as he came forward.

"Captain Stanfield! My daughter tells me you were an officer in the Peninsular wars and are here to help me with these artifacts. I am delighted, absolutely delighted! Welcome. Welcome!"

Mr. Hawthorne paused and peered through spectacles much like the ones his daughter wore. In a somewhat anxious voice he said, "You are well enough to help, are you not? You look a trifle pale."

William rose to his feet, his voice resolute as he replied, "Hello, Mr. Hawthorne. I am happy to be here and perfectly capable of assisting you, sir. I simply fell from a horse and reopened an old injury a month or so ago. I am pale from having been kept indoors while I convalesced, not from any current weakness, I assure you."

"I am glad to hear it," Mr. Hawthorne said briskly. "I cannot deny that some help with these artifacts would be most welcome." He paused and turned to his daughter. "Ariel, my dear, we shall still need someone with strong shoulders to help us move about some of the larger objects. If you could go fetch Tom, it would be of the greatest use to us."

"Of course, Papa."

When Miss Hawthorne was gone, Mr. Hawthorne looked at William and there was shrewdness in his eyes, a hint of steel in his voice, that had not been so evident before. "My daughter is an excellent assistant, and I have great respect for her abilities. I should be most displeased, Captain, if anyone were to show her the least disrespect!"

"I should not dream of doing so," William said, taken aback.

The older man relaxed. He even smiled at Stanfield. "Good. Then we understand each other. I know that ladies often have a fondness for uniforms, so I am grateful that you did not wear yours today. I trust you will continue to show such discretion in the future."

With a bitterness William had not realized he still felt, he said, "I am no longer an active soldier, sir. My injuries put paid to that. I had to sell out after I took a ball in the arm and another in my leg. The title of captain is, these days, a courtesy one."

"I, er, yes, of course," Mr. Hawthorne mumbled, clearly taken aback.

"Forgive me, sir," William said, knowing he was getting off to a bad start. "I did not mean to vent upon you my bad humor. Simply tell me where you wish to begin."

Oddly enough, Hawthorne seemed to understand. He took off his spectacles and polished them. "Too many of you came back injured. And even if you had not, I make no doubt that England would seem tame and perhaps even frivolous to you, these days. A man ought to have a purpose. What is yours, now that you can no longer be a soldier?"

William stared back. "To do what good I can."

That seemed to reassure the older man, and he nodded. "Well, you may certainly do some good here. Your help is very much needed. Perhaps we can begin with the largest pieces first. Once we have determined how and where they ought to be displayed and we have written out their provenances, we can then move on to the smaller objects."

William nodded. "And that will clear this floor faster, so that we have room to work," he suggested.

Mr. Hawthorne smiled. "Ah, you've a head on your shoulders and some common sense. Good! Can't abide a man who has none. Yes, yes, you are absolutely right. Now, come over here and tell me what this object is. That way, when my daughter returns with Tom we can have it moved into the far end of the room where it will be seen the moment anyone enters. And Ariel can take notes as we discuss the history of each piece."

William rose to his feet and came forward. When he was close to Mr. Hawthorne, he paused and shifted his cane to the hand in the sling. Then he reached into his pocket. "This might help," he told Mr. Hawthorne. "Wellington had a list drawn up of what he remembered to be here and what he knew of the object. He said he could not absolutely vouch for everything he recollects, but at least it is a starting point. I was given the list to give to you."

The other man's eyes positively gleamed with excitement. "Indeed, it is an excellent starting point," Mr. Hawthorne said as he took the pages of Wellington's list. "The moment my daughter returns, I shall set her to matching the descriptions on here to the objects."

"I thought you meant for her to take notes as we talk," William said with some amusement.

The older man waved a hand carelessly. "Oh, Ariel may do both! She is a very talented young woman, you know."

Stanfield did not have long to wonder what Miss Hawthorne would think of her father's plans for her, for she returned just then with a large man whose broad shoulders argued a strong back as well. She introduced Tom, then listened with perfect equanimity to her father's plans for her.

"Very well, Papa," she said. "Just let me fetch my writing tools."

She was back in a very short time, carrying a small writing table that had ink and quills and paper all cunningly kept secure in special places in the desk. Miss Hawthorne set it by the wall, so that she would be out of their way as they moved about, but still close enough to the two men to overhear everything that was said.

She took the list from her father and began to peruse it swiftly. It took her only a moment or two to find the description that she thought matched the object with which her father wished to begin. Captain Stanfield disagreed. He was certain it was a different object entirely. They entered into a spirited debate upon the matter, which bemused her father and upset Tom and wasted half of that first morning.

It was two days later that Mrs. Merriweather, the former governess once known as Miss Tibbles, smiled at her husband over the breakfast table. To be sure, she often did so, for Marian truly adored her Colonel Merri-weather. He was the kindest of men and made her feel, she often thought, twenty years younger.

At this precise moment, Colonel Merriweather was reading a letter and Mrs. Merriweather waited with some impatience for him to tell her what it said. To be sure, it was his letter, but the exclamations of surprise and delight with which he was reading it made her unable to ignore its importance.

"Well, sir?" she said, when he finally set the letter aside and picked up his fork to continue eating his ham.

Colonel Merriweather looked at his wife and smiled, his gaze far away as he said, "I've been invited to come to London to help organize a collection at the British Museum, m'dear."

"You?" Mrs. Merriweather blinked. "But what do you know of museum artifacts?"

The colonel bristled. "A great deal, in this case. The artifacts are from the Peninsula, from Wellington's cam-paigns, and you must know that I have as much experi-ence as anyone with what was collected there. My old friend Mr. Hawthorne has written to ask me to come and help him."

"I see."

"You would like to go to London, wouldn't you, Mar-ian dear?" Colonel Merriweather asked in a coaxing voice. "And we could bring little Elizabeth with us. My aunt is in residence in her town house and would be delighted, I am certain, to have us come for a visit."

"I see."

"Now, now, dear. I know she opposed our marriage, but you know she has been kind ever since it became a *fait accompli,*" the colonel said, correctly gauging the cause of his wife's displeasure.

Still, Mrs. Merriweather hesitated. The colonel reached across the table and took his wife's hand in his. He turned it over and lifted it up so that he could place a kiss in her palm. Then he smiled at her, an intimate smile she knew very well and loved very much.

"It will be fun," he said. "You can shop and visit friends, perhaps even some of your former charges, and I can be of service to my country."

He knew her well. Marian had begun to bristle at the suggestion that she would like filling her days with visits to shops. But the reminder that some of her former charges, from the days when she had been a governess, might be in London, and the suggestion that he could be of service to his country, were more than enough to sway her. As he knew they would be.

"Very well," she said, somewhat mollified. "Perhaps it would be a good notion to go. I just wish we need not stay with Lady Merriweather."

The colonel waved away her objections. "We need scarcely see my aunt! But Hawthorne wishes me to come at once, and there is no time to find a house for us to hire while we are in London. In any event, it is the height of the Season right now. There will not be a decent house to be had!"

Marian grumbled, but she could not deny the truth of what he said. Instead she rose to her feet and set down her napkin. "I shall go advise the staff. When do you wish to leave, my dear?"

The colonel hesitated a moment, then said briskly, "I shall send a message straight off to my aunt telling her to expect us at once. We shall leave in the morning and go by easy stages, to arrive the day after."

"And thus give Lady Merriweather no chance to refuse to house us?" Marian hazarded shrewdly.

He laughed as if she had spoken nonsense, but the red color that crept up his cheeks betrayed the truth of her words. Well, it was all the same to Marian. If Lady Merriweather refused to house them, they would just have to hire a house or stay in a hotel until they could find one. And it would not distress her in the very least to have to do so!

# 2

Ariel stared at Captain Stanfield. It bothered her that he smiled in such an animated way when he talked with her father, but seemed so stiff and formal when he spoke with her. It was not that she was unaccustomed to such treatment, but she found herself wishing for better from him. She could not have said why she was so drawn to the captain, but she was. She wished he would unbend sufficiently with her so that she could ask him about the places he had been and the things he had seen. But that seemed impossible.

It was almost, Ariel thought indignantly, as if Captain Stanfield resented her presence here. And yet the two men would be lost without her. Neither her father nor Captain Stanfield ever took time to make notes about the objects they were sorting out. That work they were quite content to leave to her. But still they treated Ariel as if she were irrelevant to them. That rankled more than she could say.

She tried to be kind to the young gentleman. She always made certain that he had a chair near to hand, in case he should grow tired. And he often used it. But he seemed to resent rather than be grateful for her kindness!

As if to prove her point, Captain Stanfield looked up at her and scowled. Her father, to make matters worse, looked up as well and said in a disapproving voice, "Are you woolgathering again, Ariel? We've no time for that!

Read me back the last notes you took of what we were saying, for I think it likely you missed something important."

The appalling thing was that when she read back her notes, Ariel discovered her father was right. She had missed the essential information that the particularly ugly object they were inspecting had come from a Spanish home that had been in itself an object of great interest, having as it did a history of Jewish and Muslim, as well as French and then British, occupation.

Hastily she tried to add the information that her father and Captain Stanfield were telling her, but suddenly her quill broke, causing her to exclaim in a most unladylike way. Her father was even less pleased.

"The devil take it, Ariel! Now we shall have to wait while you trim it or prepare a new one! Really, my dear girl, I should think you could be more careful than that."

"I may be able to be of assistance," a voice said from the far end of the hall.

"Oh, lord! More lost visitors," Mr. Hawthorne muttered under his breath. "As if we need that just now."

He turned to politely offer to show the woman to the public portion of the museum, but stopped as he recognized the man with her. "Merriweather!" he shouted.

"Hawthorne! It's wonderful to see you again. Still up to your elbows in dusty relics, ugly sculptures, and ridiculous paintings I see," the newcomer said.

With surprising agility, Mr. Hawthorne leaped to his feet and moved forward to greet his old friend. Then he turned to Captain Stanfield, completely ignoring both the woman and Ariel as he said, "I must make you known to my old friend Colonel Merriweather. But perhaps you know him already? Perhaps you met in the Peninsula? I presume you were both on Wellington's staff."

Merriweather smiled at the younger man. "Yes, of course. Good to see you again, Stanfield."

"And it's good to see you, sir. You were very highly thought of among the younger officers, you know."

Merriweather peered closer. "Heard about your injuries. Must have been worse than I was told, for I would have thought they healed long ago."

Ariel noted with interest the way Captain Stanfield colored up. He looked away from the colonel as he said gruffly, "They might have, had I not injured my arm and leg again, riding sooner than I ought to have done after my return. And another tumble a month or so ago has made it worse than ever."

Someone cleared her throat, rather ostentatiously, and as if surprised to be recalled to her existence, all three men turned to the woman with Colonel Merriweather. He colored up and said hastily, "May I present my wife, Mrs. Merriweather? My dear, this is my old friend Mr. Hawthorne, and a fellow officer, Captain Stanfield."

She smiled a thin smile but looked beyond them and afforded a truly cordial smile to Ariel. She moved past the men and walked straight up to the younger woman.

"No use expecting them to think to introduce us. I collect you've a problem; perhaps I may be of help? I'm a dab hand at trimming quills."

Ariel smiled, despite herself, at the woman's odd manners. "Thank you. I am Miss Hawthorne. And I should be grateful for any assistance you can give me. Papa gets most impatient when I cannot take notes for him."

"He does, does he?" Mrs. Merriweather said, regarding Ariel's father with a shrewd eye. "Very well; then I shall help you. For while you may have been able to write down everything important that your father and this young man said, now that my husband is here to help, the work will increase greatly, I assure you. With my help, we may take turns and you need not find yourself quite so overwhelmed."

Ariel could not quite decide whether to be grateful for the offer of assistance or insulted that the woman thought she could not manage on her own. But then, she had not managed on her own, even with just her father and Captain Stanfield, and that was what had led to the problem with her quill.

"You might as well not argue," the colonel said, coming up to stand behind his wife. He placed a hand on her waist and smiled at Ariel. There was a distinct twinkle in his eyes as he said, "My wife, Mrs. Merriweather, used to be a governess and is therefore accustomed to both being of service and getting her own way."

In spite of herself, Ariel laughed. "Very well, then, Mrs. Merriweather. I shall be very grateful for your assistance. I will find another chair, more quills and paper, and we may both share this little desk between us."

"No, no. Tom, go fetch a small table," Mr. Hawthorne told their worker. "Anything about the height of Ariel's desk will do."

Tom, who had been sitting in the shadows, waiting until his strength was needed to move something, now came forward and nodded his understanding. Then he headed off to fetch the requested table.

To the newcomers, Mr. Hawthorne explained, "Tom's a simple fellow, but I'll swear he knows more about what's in this museum than I do. He'll fetch a table, and faster than I could, I'll vow. Ah, here he comes now. You see? Now we may all be comfortable. Yes, yes, put it there, Tom. Merriweather, come see what we've got."

Ariel looked at Mrs. Merriweather, who had already found herself a chair and drawn it up close. She had also removed her gloves and was reaching for a quill and the knife with which to sharpen it. "Are you quite certain you wish to do this?" Ariel asked with some hesitation. "I cannot think it kind of us to put you to work this way."

The older woman merely looked at her, brows raised, and said, "My dear, when you are better acquainted with me, you will discover that I despise sitting idle. There is nothing I like better than to be of use, so long as it *is* of use and not merely something thought up to keep me busy. Here, Miss Hawthorne. I believe you will find this quill satisfactory, and I shall just take a moment to trim another for myself. Then, if you will give me some paper, I may take over for a bit and you may rest. When I become tired, you may take over for me."

Mrs. Merriweather was as good as her word, and within moments she was writing, attempting to keep up with what the men were saying, and Ariel could sit back and simply watch. Of course, it wasn't watching that Ariel truly wished to do. What she would have liked was to sit on the floor with her father, sorting through the objects, asking her own questions of Captain Stanfield and Colonel Merriweather.

Somehow, without meaning to do so, at some point the wish became reality and Ariel found herself kneeling next to Captain Stanfield. "Why does this look so much like a cooking pot?" she asked.

"Because it was," he answered promptly.

"Nonsense! Why would anyone have brought back a cooking pot?" her father demanded impatiently.

Captain Stanfield smiled, and it was, in Ariel's opinion, a singularly sweet and wistful smile. "Because Wellington wanted everything to be remembered. Not just the spoils of war, but the day-to-day privations as well. He wishes those who come to the museum to see what it was like for us, in the Peninsula. Not some elegant dinner party meals, but food cooked in one pot with whatever we could find to put in it, heated with whatever we could find to burn for fuel."

Colonel Merriweather nodded. "Aye, it was very different from what I've discovered the people back home imagined. It is just like the Duke of Wellington to want the public to see it all."

Mr. Hawthorne shook his head. "Very well, but it makes much more work this way. And I cannot guarantee that we will ever have sufficient room to display it all. The paintings and sculpture, yes, of course room will be made for them. But the rest . . ."

Others might have thought her father was complaining, but Ariel recognized his expression as one of pleasure. Papa liked nothing better than to have lots of things to sort through and make notes about and plan exhibits around. No, he was not complaining but rather settling in for what he expected to be a most satisfying job.

"This you might find to be of greater interest than a cooking pot, Miss Hawthorne," Stanfield said quietly.

She turned to see him holding a necklace. "It's beautiful!" Ariel said, reaching out to take the piece. "But some poor woman has lost something she must have treasured."

Her father made a dismissive sound. "No doubt she had a great many more like it. Women always do! No, no, concentrate, Ariel! Concentrate on the things that matter, like the pistols and swords. I should like to place them so that we may show the contrast between French and British and Spanish swords and pistols."

"Yes, Papa."

Ariel did as her father had asked, helping the men pull what was wanted out of the pile with the weapons. But her eyes strayed more than once to the necklace Captain Stanfield had shown her. And her thoughts went more than once to the kindness in his nature that had prompted him to do so. It must have been kindness, for why else would he have done so? It was the first evidence she had seen that he did not entirely view her with contempt, and Ariel clung to it.

It was nearly two o'clock in the afternoon when Mr. Hawthorne agreed to allow them all to take a short break. It was Mrs. Merriweather who pointed out to him that she and Ariel, at least, were in need of sustenance.

"To be sure; to be sure," Mr. Hawthorne hastily agreed. "Here, Tom, here are some funds. Go round to the usual place and bring back enough food for five people."

"Enough food for six people, Papa," Ariel corrected him gently.

Hawthorne blinked, then realized she was counting Tom. "Oh, er, yes, of course. You must eat as well, Tom. Fetch enough for six," he said.

Tom nodded, took the coins, and with a huge grin sped out of the hall. Hawthorne turned to Colonel Merriweather. "While we are waiting for Tom to return, I have something in my office I should like to show you," he said.

"Yes, of course," Merriweather said.

It was one of the things Hawthorne liked most about his old friend—he did not ask questions; he simply came. When they got there, Hawthorne shut the door and turned to the colonel. He removed his spectacles and took a moment or two to polish them. Then he took a deep breath and said, "I didn't ask you to come to the museum simply because I need help with sorting out these objects, although I do. I also asked you to come because there is a problem here at the museum and I couldn't think whom else to ask for help. Not without risking a scandal the museum can ill afford."

"What's going on?" Merriweather asked. "Theft?"

Hawthorne started. "How did you—"

He stopped himself and waited. After a moment, Merriweather sighed. "I cannot help you, Richard, unless you are honest with me about what is going on. I made a guess that it might be theft because it seemed the most obvious possibility."

Hawthorne began to pace about the small room. "Yes, yes, I know you are right," he admitted. "And yet, I am reluctant to speak about it to anyone. But if I don't, matters will get even worse. And you are discreet. I know you are. I haven't forgotten that little matter when we were at school together and Winslow ran into trouble. And I know that I sent for you, but now that you are here, I find myself unable to decide how best to broach the subject."

"Begin at the beginning," Merriweather advised. When Hawthorne still did not explain, the colonel tried another approach. "Let me make some guesses, and you can tell me if I've hit the mark or not. You've already let slip that theft may be involved. I must presume that you have not called in the Bow Street Runners, or you would not need me. Do you perhaps suspect someone who works at the museum?"

Hawthorne seemed to go even paler than before. "It would be a catastrophe, were that to be the case," he said, avoiding Merriweather's eyes.

"And you don't wish to suspect anyone you work with anyway, do you? Or to make accusations without absolute proof," Merriweather hazarded shrewdly. "But if not someone who works here, then who else could it be? One of the visitors to the museum? If so, it would have to be someone who knows the place well and has found a means to enter after hours, for I presume the guard at the gate would notice someone attempting to take things out during the day. Is there anyone who has shown an unusual interest in the museum?"

"There are so many visitors that I cannot say whether anyone has been here often or not, or shown an unusual interest," Hawthorne said irritably, still avoiding Merriweather's gaze.

"Do you have a night watchman?" the colonel asked, suppressing his own irritation.

"T-tom serves as our night watchman," Hawthorne said reluctantly. "But no one really expects him to do anything. It's really only a reason to let him sleep here. Theft, at night, has never been a problem before, you see."

Merriweather tried another approach. "Suppose the theft or thefts occurred after hours; then it would have to be someone with a key or keys to the museum. Which would argue that it is indeed someone who works here. How many have the necessary key or keys?"

Hawthorne stiffened. "I am the only one with the authority to carry all the keys that would be needed to get into the museum at night."

It was not quite an answer, but Merriweather let it pass. "Perhaps someone has picked the locks?" he suggested.

"Perhaps. But I've seen no signs of tampering nor broken windows to explain any other way the thief or thieves could have gotten in."

The colonel began to lose his temper. "Look, if you

do not mean to tell me more than this, then why did you ask me to come and help?" he demanded.

Hawthorne shrugged. "I didn't know what else to do," he admitted reluctantly. "I trust your intelligence and your common sense and your discretion, and that's more than I can say for anyone else. And it was particularly convenient because I had such a good excuse to call you in."

"Only now you find that you cannot make up your mind how much to tell me," Merriweather suggested, a tinge of bitterness in his voice.

Hawthorne nodded unhappily. "I did not expect it to be so difficult, but it is! Bear with me a day or two, while I make up my mind, will you?" he asked.

The colonel wanted to refuse, but he didn't. In the end, he clapped Hawthorne on the shoulder and said, "Very well. We have been friends too long for me to refuse."

Hawthorne let out a sigh of relief.

Neither of them noticed the young man who slipped away before they could discover him listening at the door. Neither of them noticed that Captain Stanfield returned to the room where they were working just moments before they did so. After all, it would never have occurred to Colonel Merriweather or Mr. Hawthorne that he could have been nearby without either of them hearing the distinctive sound of his cane on the hardwood floors.

# 3

"What, my dear, was that all about with Mr. Hawthorne?" Mrs. Merriweather asked the colonel when they finally left the museum for the day.

"Er, what do you mean?" he countered, as he handed her into their carriage.

She sighed as she settled herself. "You really ought to know by now, my dear, that I am not stupid. Mr. Hawthorne took you into his office to talk for a reason. I am simply asking what that reason might have been."

The colonel frowned. "If Mr. Hawthorne had wished you to know, he would have told you himself. And after your last adventure, I do not want you involved in anything dangerous ever again."

She turned to him with eyes wide open. "So there *is* a mystery here!" Marian exclaimed.

"I did not say so!" he all but growled.

"You do not have to say so," Mrs. Merriweather said with some satisfaction. "It is evident from what you will not say. Now, I wonder what it could be. . . . Theft, I should think. That would be the most likely sort of crime to occur in a museum. It cannot be murder, for if that were the case he would have called in a Bow Street Runner. But a mere theft, yes, he might trust you to help him with that. Though I must say that I do not understand why he would be reluctant to call in a Bow Street Runner for that as well."

The colonel bristled. "Really, Marian, this habit of yours of knowing far too much is not at all the way one expects a lady to behave."

"I am who I am, and you married me just the same," Mrs. Merriweather said placidly.

"So I did, but that does not mean I cannot wish for a little more decorum from time to time," he countered.

"You may wish for whatever you like," she conceded generously, "so long as you do not expect to get it."

What more the colonel might have said went unspoken, for they had reached Lady Merriweather's town house and they were late. She had arranged a dinner party in their honor, and they would scarcely have time to clean off the dirt of the day and change into evening clothes before the first guests would arrive. That Lady Merriweather felt the full force of this solecism was evident from the expression on her majordomo's face as he let them in, and in the fact that as they climbed the stairs up toward the room that had been put at their disposal, Lady Merriweather stepped into the hallway and accosted them.

"This is what you consider an appropriate time to come home to dress for dinner?" Lady Merriweather demanded. "And covered with dirt, at that. Are those ink stains on your wife's fingers? Do you have no consideration for my feelings or the effort to which I have gone on your behalf?"

The colonel drew himself up to his full height. "My dear Aunt Cordelia, you must have had this dinner party organized long before we appeared on your doorstep, for there would have been no time to do so since we arrived. It is kind of you to pretend it is for us, but you know very well your guests are coming for the pleasure of your company and they will scarcely know we are here."

"Oh, they will notice you are here," she countered, a trifle bitterly. "And remember only too well that your wife was once a governess. I had hoped to give them no further cause for gossip. That is obviously hopeless."

"Quite hopeless," Marian agreed. "I wonder, then, given the lateness of the hour, that you delay us even further."

Lady Merriweather glared at her nephew's wife, but she stepped aside so that they could continue on their way upstairs. Behind them, she called out one parting shot. "Your daughter dumped a bucket of water all over her nurse this afternoon. I don't think she is very happy here!"

Captain Stanfield watched as Miss Hawthorne packed up her things. He worried about her. She looked exhausted, and he was certain that her father would neither notice nor particularly care. In spite of his resolve to keep his distance, he could not help but say, "You need not have stayed so late, Miss Hawthorne. Your father and I could have continued this work on our own."

She shook her head. "Who would have taken notes? You cannot, not when your right arm is injured like that. And Papa is hopeless at doing so."

William hesitated, then found himself asking impulsively, "Do you not mind being used in such a way? Particularly as I cannot think your father ever gives a thought to your comfort."

There was a wistful look in Miss Hawthorne's eyes behind those spectacles that always seemed a trifle precariously placed on the bridge of her nose. But when she answered, it was with a brisk air of composure. "I wish to be here, at the museum, and in helping my father I am able to do so. I cannot think the price so very high. Indeed, I think it would be worth almost any price to be able to be around such wonderful things all day long."

He wanted to press the point, but instead he reminded himself that this was not why he was here. Never mind that he wished he could see Miss Hawthorne laughing and carefree. That was not his affair. He had a task to focus on, and it was time he did so again!

So now Captain Stanfield smiled at Miss Hawthorne, a trifle distantly this time. His voice was cool as he said, "I see. Very well. In any event, I am grateful to you, Miss Hawthorne, for your assistance. But now, I suppose I had better go find your father and discover at what time he wishes me to arrive tomorrow. He said something about a meeting and that I might not be needed until later than usual."

Then, with a smile and a bow, he left her. Stanfield leaned heavily on his cane—at least until he was out of sight. Then he suddenly became surprisingly agile as he slipped around a corner and listened for voices. He heard one he recognized and followed it until he found Mr. Hawthorne talking with a gentleman William didn't know. By the time they noticed him, the limp was as pronounced as ever, his cane landed loudly on the hardwood floor with each step again, and Stanfield looked every bit the exhausted young veteran he purported to be.

At the sight of him, the other two men broke off their conversation and Mr. Hawthorne hurried to William's side. "Here, now, Captain Stanfield! You ought not to have exerted yourself in such a way," Hawthorne protested. "I would have come and found you shortly. Or you could have sent my daughter to find me."

"I didn't wish to put either of you to such trouble," William said with a wan smile as he sat down on the chair Hawthorne urged him toward.

"Nonsense! It would have been good for Ariel! Now, what did you wish to speak to me about?"

Stanfield hesitated. "It seems foolish now, but I meant to ask at what hour you needed me tomorrow. I had intended to arrive at the usual time, even if you expected to be busy, but I think perhaps I've put myself to a greater strain than I anticipated. Now I find that I must ask whether you would mind if I went, in the morning, to see a surgeon and came at noon instead."

"My dear boy, I shouldn't mind at all!" Mr. Haw-

thorne said with some hint of alarm in his voice. "I had
no notion we were working you so hard. You ought to
have told me it was too much for you."

Stanfield waved a hand. "I shall be fine. I simply need
to be a little more careful. I am only sorry to disappoint
you this way."

"I am not in the least disappointed in you," Hawthorne countered. "You have been of the greatest assistance. Come, I'll help you out to the street and find a
hackney to take you home." He paused and turned to
speak to the other man who had been silent through all
of this. "I shall be back shortly and we may talk some
more then."

Hawthorne was as good as his word, and William soon
found himself headed for the rooms he had hired years
ago. They were not at a fashionable address, nor particularly elegant, but they would do. In any event, he was
often away, and it was, he told himself firmly, far better
than staying at his parents' town house and having both
his mother, and even his sisters on their frequent visits,
badgering him to marry. It was useless to point out that
he was a younger son and his marriage couldn't possibly
signify to anyone. But once his mother and sisters took
a notion in their heads, there was no turning them from
it. Far better to live in shabby rooms he scarcely noticed
than subject himself to that nonsense!


In the museum, in her father's office, Ariel stared at
the piles of papers and books and artifacts that covered
every free surface. One of these days she really ought to
try to organize things for him. But she had tried that
once before, and he had not been in the least grateful
to her for doing so. She sighed. It was not that she was
precisely unhappy, but this was not quite how she had
envisioned her life either.

There had been a time when she had dreamed the
same sort of dreams for herself that every young woman
dreams. A time when she had thought that someday she

might find someone to love. The past few years had taught her how foolish such dreams were—at least for her.

Naturally, her father chose precisely that moment to return. "Is something wrong, my dear?" his concerned voice came from the doorway.

Ariel turned away briefly and then back to greet her father, a smile now fixed as firmly in place as her spectacles. "No, of course not, Papa. I am just tired, I suppose." She paused, then added, "Captain Stanfield seemed tired as well."

Hawthorne came forward and peered anxiously into his daughter's face, but then seemed to take her at her word. He sighed. "I must admit that I am somewhat concerned about Captain Stanfield. He seems very weak. One would have thought that so many years after the war was over, he would be stronger by now. No doubt his recent tumble from a horse has made matters worse, but I suspect the truth is that the war ruined his constitution, and we must make allowances for that and take care not to press him too hard."

"I think you may be right. But I am also concerned with how tired *you* appear to be, Papa," Ariel countered. "Won't you come home with me now?"

He hesitated, and then shook his head. "You go ahead," he said. "There are some things I must finish up here first. But I shall be along as soon as I have."

Ariel wanted to refuse. But she didn't. She knew her father too well to think he could be swayed, once he had made up his mind.

"Very well, Papa. I shall see you at home. Please do not stay too late."

He nodded and let her go. Ariel did not see, nor did Hawthorne, the man who lurked behind the half-open door and who quickly slipped out of sight as she gathered her things. Nor did she notice him watching as she climbed into a hackney to head for home.

\*     \*     \*

It was late, very late, when Stanfield entered a nonde-script building in a nondescript part of town. He had intended to come in the morning, but the note delivered to his rooms summoned him here tonight.

By the time he reached the top of the stairs, the door was open to the office he sought. Thornsby, the man who had summoned Stanfield, wasted no time waving him to a seat.

"Well? You have been there a week. What news?" Thornsby asked.

"I am in place, and everyone takes me to be the in-valid I seem to be," William said with no little satisfac-tion. "I am trusted and may move about as I wish."

"No one suspects you?"

William shook his head. "I am perceived to be a harm-less fellow."

"Very good. And you are making progress? Have you found a way to stay in the museum overnight?"

"Not yet. I am still feeling my way. But Hawthorne and his daughter trust me. She is his assistant, by the by. And the clerks and other scholars there have also be-come accustomed to the sight of me. But there is some-one I should like to know more about. A man named Colonel Merriweather arrived today. I knew him in the Peninsula and he was well thought of there. Hawthorne asked him to come and help sort out the artifacts."

"So?" Thornsby asked.

William hesitated. "They were closeted together for a time this afternoon, Hawthorne and Merriweather. I tried to overhear what was said, but without much suc-cess. I should like to know if Colonel Merriweather poses a threat to what you wish me to do."

The other man nodded. "I'll find out and send you word as soon as I can. Meanwhile, continue as you have. There is a great deal of money to be made, stealing from the museum, but only if everyone plays his cards just right. So keep your eyes open and your wits about you!"

William nodded. There was a grim look about his eyes

and mouth. "I shall," he said. "I've no desire to add any more wounds to the ones I already have."

"You go armed?" the other man asked.

William grimaced and drew the pistol out of the sling. "Everywhere," he said. "Nothing and no one shall stop me from my purpose."

"Good. You had better go now. I am expecting someone else soon. You had best go out the back way."

William nodded, rising to his feet at once. He moved silently and with a grace and skill that belied the injuries that seemed so evident during the day. Nor was there any trace of diffidence in his manner. Had the Merriweathers or the Hawthornes chanced to see him now, they would have been very surprised indeed.

# 4

Ariel arrived at the museum some time after her father. He had come home so late and then been gone when she woke that morning, and it worried her, for he was keeping more and more secrets lately. And that was not like him. Her father had always been the most open of men. It worried her that he did not seem to feel he could tell her what he was doing, what it was that kept him so preoccupied these days. It had something to do with the museum, she was sure, for that was all she sometimes thought he cared about. But beyond that she knew nothing except that sometimes he came home after she was asleep, or left before she woke. And on such days his face always seemed lined with worry.

As she stepped down from the carriage, she bumped against someone, nearly knocking the spectacles off her nose. She turned to find Captain Stanfield reaching out his good hand to steady her. It was very early, even for her to be here, and certainly well before the time of noon that Captain Stanfield had told her father to expect him. He seemed equally taken aback to find her there so early.

"I thought you were not coming until later," she said.

He seemed to color up. "I, er, the surgeon could not see me this morning, so I thought I might as well come along and see if there was anything I could do to help. You are here remarkably early yourself."

Before she could answer, before she could decide

whether or not to confide in him her fears concerning
her father, another carriage arrived and deposited Colonel and Mrs. Merriweather right beside them. Ariel could
not decide whether she felt relieved or disappointed.

They had begun the customary round of greetings,
when suddenly a sound came from the direction of the
museum. Tom stood in the doorway, shouting something
unintelligible but betraying his distress. They all hurried
toward him, and he promptly disappeared back into
the museum.

It was in the hall where they had been working that
they found Ariel's father. He lay facedown among the
artifacts they had been sorting through the day before.
And he was unmistakably dead, stabbed with a Moorish-
looking dagger that had been one of the spoils of war
brought back from the Peninsula and donated to the
museum.

To Ariel, it was as if the voices of the others came
from a distance. Instinctively she reached out to grasp
onto something, but there was nothing nearby. She heard
the clatter of the captain's cane falling to the floor, and
then a strong arm came around her waist, holding her up.

"Courage," Captain Stanfield's voice came from beside her.

"Are you faint?" Colonel Merriweather demanded.
"There is a chair over here. I shall get it for you."

He was as good as his word. He brought over the chair
and helped her sit down in it. Ariel was grateful for his
solicitude and for the captain's. "Is Papa really dead?"
she asked, knowing what the answer was but some part
of her still hoping she was wrong.

Captain Stanfield placed an encouraging hand on her
shoulder. "Yes," he said.

And then Mrs. Merriweather knelt beside Ariel, peering closely at her face. The older woman's voice was
steady but gentle as she asked, "Do you have any relatives, my dear? Anyone we could send for to come and
be with you?"

Ariel shook her head. Her voice was strained as she

replied, "Papa had no family. Nor did Mama. None that I know of, at any rate."

The colonel's voice intruded now as he said softly to his wife, "Hawthorne was the last of his line, and his wife was an orphan. That was the reason he could indulge his fancy and come to work at the museum. No one to stop him, you see."

"What about friends?" Captain Stanfield suggested.

"Papa had friends, but I did not know them very well," Ariel replied. "As for me, I-I have none. I was too different from the other girls my age, and while Papa's friends would be kind, I do not think I could ask any of them to stay in the house with me. Papa scorned the notion of propriety, but I find I cannot be quite so casual about it as he was."

"I should think not!" Mrs. Merriweather said indignantly. Her voice took on a hint of urgency as she persisted. "If I were to escort you home, Miss Hawthorne, would your housekeeper be there? A maid? Or anyone?"

Ariel shook her head again. "Papa kept no household staff. He thought it a useless indulgence. There was a woman who would come to clean at times, but today is not her day. We sent our laundry out, and I did all the cooking."

The colonel patted her hand awkwardly. "You must be brave, my dear," he said. To the others he said, "We shall have to send for a Bow Street Runner. Perhaps Tom could go."

"No! You cannot send Tom," Ariel protested. "He must already be upset at having found my father this way. In any event, he would find it much too hard to explain what has happened in a way that a Bow Street Runner would understand."

That gave the colonel pause. He turned and looked at Tom, who was shifting his weight back and forth, his face clearly contorted with distress. "Yes, of course," the colonel said quietly. "Quite right you are, Miss Hawthorne. Stanfield, perhaps you would be so good as to go to Bow Street and fetch a Runner?"

"Of course."

"Good. But be careful as you go back through the museum," the colonel warned. "Hawthorne looks to have been dead for some time, but I could be mistaken. And one wouldn't want to startle the person who did this and have him attack you!"

As Tom sat down on the floor and began rocking back and forth in distress, Ariel watched Captain Stanfield move from the room as swiftly as his injured leg would permit.

The colonel and Mrs. Merriweather began to discuss her situation, but Ariel could not bring herself to greatly care. Still, she listened.

"We must do something for Miss Hawthorne," Mrs. Merriweather said in a low voice. "You heard her say that she has no relatives, nor even a household staff, to be of support to her right now. Perhaps we should stay with her?"

"What would my aunt think of that?" the colonel asked impatiently. "And who would look after Elizabeth? There will be no one at the Hawthorne house who could do so. You surely are not suggesting we leave our daughter behind?"

Mrs. Merriweather sighed. "No, of course not. I am simply worried about Miss Hawthorne."

"Well, and so am I," the colonel agreed. "That is why I shall arrange for someone to stay at the house with her. Perhaps a couple, a husband and wife, who can watch over things and help to deal with all the funeral arrangements that must be made. But first we must speak with the Bow Street Runner."

"Yes, and before he gets here someone should see what they can puzzle out about this murder," Mrs. Merriweather said roundly.

The colonel snorted. And then he said, with no little exasperation, "I suppose this means, Marian, that you are going to insist upon being a part of all of this? Even though you know that I do not like the notion of you being involved with death again."

Mrs. Merriweather regarded her husband with a withering expression as she retorted, "It was not my notion to come to London and meddle at the British Museum. Mr. Hawthorne was your friend, not mine. But since I am here, you cannot keep me out of things."

The colonel grumbled; he distinctly grumbled. Marian did not let it deter her. She glanced at Miss Hawthorne. The young woman seemed stunned, but not about to faint. Good. Marian could turn her attention back to her husband.

"I think you had better tell me everything that Mr. Hawthorne told you yesterday," she said briskly, though so softly that she hoped Miss Hawthorne would not overhear her. "I thought at the time that it must be something important, and it seems I was right."

"I don't like this, Marian," the colonel repeated.

Mrs. Merriweather nodded toward the body. "I suspect Mr. Hawthorne likes it even less. But now that there has been a murder, the best thing you can do is share with me whatever you know and let the two of us work together to resolve the problem."

"Hawthorne spoke to me in confidence."

"And now you will tell me in confidence."

"It is not proper."

Mrs. Merriweather drew herself up to her full diminutive height. "I was a governess for twenty years, my dear," she said with some asperity. "I think I may know something of what is proper and what is not, and murder is always improper! The need to discover who did this surely outweighs all other considerations."

"It might not be safe!"

Marian Merriweather simply regarded her husband with a steady gaze. Thus reminded of the many adventures that she had already endured, he flushed a bright red and muttered, "Well, you cannot expect me to like seeing you placed in even the slightest danger."

She reached out and placed a hand over his. "Nor can

you expect me to like the notion of you being in danger," she retorted gently.

For a moment he caught her hand in his. Then the colonel cleared his throat and said briskly, "I shall tell you later, my dear. You may find it is far less useful than you expect. For now, we should see what we can determine before the Runner arrives."

Marian nodded, recognizing the wisdom in what the colonel suggested. So now they both studied the body carefully and all the space around it. In quiet voices they pointed out to each other what they saw. By the time the Runner, a Mr. Collins, arrived, they were ready to discuss matters with him.

"It is Mr. Hawthorne, the curator here at the museum, who is dead," Mrs. Merriweather told the Runner as he stared at the body, though she was certain Captain Stanfield must have already done so. Still, it did not hurt to repeat information for these fellows.

As though to forestall his wife's efforts to include herself in the investigation, the colonel hastily jumped in and began to tell Collins what they had concluded.

"Hawthorne was obviously stabbed and then dragged here from somewhere else," Colonel Merriweather said.

"Oh? 'e were, were 'e? And where might that somewhere else 'ave been?" the Runner asked, not troubling to hide the sarcasm in his voice.

The colonel stiffened. "I don't know," he admitted. "One can see that the body was dragged into this room, because the floor was dusty and one can see the trail that was left. But elsewhere the floors were swept clean, and any blood that spilled must have been wiped up. Still, he was dragged from deeper in the museum, since that is the doorway through which his body came."

The colonel began to point out to Mr. Collins what he and Mrs. Merriweather had discovered. The Runner made notes to himself and then placed the notebook in his breast pocket.

" 'Oos to pay me for me time?" the fellow from Bow Street asked.

"I will," Miss Hawthorne said, rising to her feet and coming toward the group around her father's body. "I suspect that Papa didn't leave me much money, but I will happily use whatever there is to discover who killed him."

"I'll pay," Captain Stanfield said, looking very pale, as though the trip to Bow Street and back had cost him too much of his precarious stamina. "I've more money than I know how to spend, thanks to a generous uncle."

"No, I'll pay," Colonel Merriweather said grimly. "Hawthorne asked me to come help him, and obviously I failed to do anything of the sort. It is therefore my responsibility to help him now."

There was a cacophony of voices arguing the matter, but the Runner made his own choice. He turned to the colonel and briskly negotiated his fee. Then he eyed the entire group and said, "I'd best be checking the rest of the museum. Seeing if I can see where the genl'mun might of been killed."

"I'll go with you," the colonel said. "And perhaps we should take Tom. He knows this building as well as anyone, other than Miss Hawthorne, of course."

The Runner nodded. The colonel went over to the young man and touched his shoulder. Tom stopped rocking. In a gentle voice the colonel said, "We shall want your help, Tom. You need to show us about the museum. It's what Mr. Hawthorne would have wanted."

That was enough for Tom. He quickly came to his feet. "I'll show you. Show you whatever you want," he said. "For Mr. Hawthorne."

After the three men left the room, Captain Stanfield said something to Miss Hawthorne and then came over to Mrs. Merriweather. In a quiet voice he said, "Miss Hawthorne cannot stay here. But I do not like the notion that she will be going back to an empty house."

"Nor I," Mrs. Merriweather agreed. "That is why I mean to stay with her until the colonel can make the arrangements for someone else to be at the house with her. He has promised to do so as quickly as possible."

Stanfield let out a sigh of relief. "I am glad to hear it. I worry about how fragile she seems."

Together they went over to the younger woman and tried to persuade her to come with them. She did not wish to leave her father, but in the end she agreed to do so when Mrs. Merriweather and Captain Stanfield assured her that Colonel Merriweather would see to it that the body was brought to her house as soon as possible.

Miss Hawthorne looked a trifle dazed, for which Mrs. Merriweather could not blame her. But the sooner they were out of the museum the better; so Marian took Miss Hawthorne's arm and started toward the doorway of the room. She noted approvingly that the captain stayed at Miss Hawthorne's other side and spoke to her in low, soothing tones.

Within minutes they found themselves outside the museum and climbing into the Merriweathers' carriage. The coachman listened as Captain Stanfield gave him directions, then set off at a brisk pace the moment they were all settled inside.

The house to which the driver took them was in a shabby but genteel part of town that catered to ladies and gentlemen who might not have had the funds to move in the first circles, but who were still ladies and gentlemen. This, of course, came as no surprise to Marian. The colonel had already told her how his friend had been so enamored of books that he had become the despair of his family. That he had been born a gentleman and married a lady, but involved himself so deeply in research and the British Museum that he might as well have resigned his designation as such.

It was evident that it was something of a shock to Captain Stanfield to discover that Miss Hawthorne might not be the daughter of a cit, as he had presumed. Which, on the whole, Mrs. Merriweather thought with an inward smile, was not necessarily such a bad thing.

Marian said none of this aloud. Indeed, she seemed quite content to follow behind the youngsters as they went into the house.

Miss Hawthorne gasped in dismay when she reached her father's study. Instantly, Captain Stanfield and Mrs. Merriweather were at her side asking what was wrong, for she had gone very pale and there was no mistaking the distress in her voice.

"Papa's books!" Miss Hawthorne said, stepping forward into the room.

That was when Captain Stanfield and Mrs. Merriweather realized they were not simply looking at the natural disorder of the library of a scholar, but a room that had been thoroughly searched. As Miss Hawthorne moved past the window, a figure suddenly darted out from behind the draperies. Before Stanfield could move to stop him, or Mrs. Merriweather could even move out of the way, the fellow had shoved past, knocking them both to the ground. He was out the front door before Stanfield could get to his feet, and in any event, Mrs. Merriweather seemed a trifle dazed and in need of his attention.

Miss Hawthorne quickly knelt beside the former governess. "Are you all right?" she asked.

Mrs. Merriweather sat up slowly and looked at Captain Stanfield. "Are you all right, sir?" she countered. "Perhaps you ought to sit down. You look as shaken as I feel."

"I am fine," he said, his voice curt with suppressed anger.

But Miss Hawthorne now took up the cause as well. She looked at him with obvious concern and said, "Are you certain? You may have injured your arm or your leg again."

Stanfield took a deep breath and visibly made an effort to hold on to his temper. "I cannot sit down," he explained shortly, "until I have made certain that the rest of the house is safe. Stay behind me, both of you, or better yet, stay in this room. Close the door when I leave and lock it, Miss Hawthorne, if you have a key. Open it again only to me."

Both women looked at him doubtfully, but it was Miss

Hawthorne who acted. She shook her head. And with what Captain Stanfield found to be most unladylike resolution, she marched over to her father's desk, opened a drawer, reached under a pile of papers, and pulled out a pistol.

"Good. He did not find this," she said with obvious satisfaction.

"Put that pistol down!" Stanfield said with some alarm. "You do not know if it is loaded."

She looked at him in surprise. "Of course it is loaded," she said. "Papa always kept it loaded."

"All the more reason to put it down," Stanfield said grimly. "Either that or give it to me."

Miss Hawthorne shook her head. "No. You've only one good arm and you need it for your cane. I shall follow behind you and hold on to the pistol. You needn't fear that I shan't know how to use it, for Papa made certain I did, some years ago. He wished, you see, to be certain that I could protect myself against impertinences."

"Impertinences." Captain Stanfield ground out the word from between clenched teeth. "I should say this goes far beyond impertinence!"

Miss Hawthorne merely regarded him with a steady gaze, and Stanfield gave an audible sigh of defeat. She thought him all but helpless, and he could not tell her otherwise without betraying more than was prudent. No, for now he had no choice but to let her continue to believe as she did. And that meant allowing her to keep hold of the pistol. He only hoped she would not end up putting a shot into his back if she tripped on the stairs or someone startled them!

Still, he tried. "What about Mrs. Merriweather?" he asked. "Surely you should stay and guard her."

That caused Miss Hawthorne to hesitate. Particularly as Mrs. Merriweather, for her own reasons, did not disagree with the captain. "I suppose I should protect her," Miss Hawthorne said reluctantly. "But what about you?"

It went against the grain, but Stanfield said, "If need be, I shall call out and you can come to my rescue."

"Very well," Miss Hawthorne agreed reluctantly. "But you must call out at once! I will not have it on my conscience that you were hurt when I might, with a little more resolution, have prevented it."

Without another word, Stanfield rose to his feet and slowly started toward the door of the parlor. He paused to check behind the other draperies in the room, but apparently there had only been one intruder here. The rest of the house was another matter, and he would not rest secure until he had checked every room of it. Slowly he began the task.

Fifteen minutes later, he was back in Hawthorne's study and he and the women were sitting on chairs facing one another.

"There seems to be no one else in the house," William said with some relief.

"But why was anyone here?" Miss Hawthorne asked, looking around the room, an expression of helplessness upon her face. "What could anyone have thought to find? It is not as if Papa ever brought anything home. And surely no one could have thought he had money! One has only to look at us to know we do not."

"Well, whatever the reason, clearly you cannot stay here," Captain Stanfield said.

Miss Hawthorne started to protest, but Mrs. Merriweather cut her short. "The captain is quite correct. It is not safe for you to stay. Not even if the colonel arranges for someone to be here with your father's body. You will stay with me at Lady Merriweather's town house."

"And what will Lady Merriweather think of having a houseguest thrust upon her unexpectedly?" Miss Hawthorne asked tartly.

"Lady Merriweather will think whatever she chooses to think," Marian countered. "My concern is for your safety, and in this I will not be swayed."

"Come. You must see that you cannot stay here," Stanfield said in a coaxing tone of voice.

Still, Miss Hawthorne hesitated. "But what about my father? I ought to be here watching over his body," she said, her voice breaking as she said the words.

The former governess patted her hand. "Your father would want you to be safe, my dear. As for your father's body, I have already told you that the colonel is arranging for someone to be here with it."

She was going to argue further, to use this as a reason to stay, but Mrs. Merriweather forestalled her. "I assure you, Miss Hawthorne, whomever the colonel hires for the task will find it easier to look after your father's body if you are not here needing to be guarded as well."

In the end, Miss Hawthorne allowed herself to be persuaded. She moved about the small house packing up essentials to take with her while Captain Stanfield stood nearby.

As for Mrs. Merriweather, anyone watching would have very likely said that the former governess merely wandered about, looking with vapid curiosity, at all the rooms of the house. Only those who knew her well would have realized how carefully Marian was studying the place. Only someone watching closely would have realized how swiftly but thoroughly she managed to search those places she decided to search.

Perhaps it was that she was so distracted she simply didn't care, but in record time Miss Hawthorne was ready to leave. Captain Stanfield would have tried to carry her valises, if she had let him. Instead, she and Mrs. Merriweather managed the baggage between them, scolding the young man for his foolishness in trying to do more than was wise, given the state of his arm and leg.

Marian half expected Captain Stanfield to take his leave of them once they were quit of the house, but he did not. Instead he quietly told them that he would see them all the way to Lady Merriweather's house. And if it were not too much trouble, he would prefer to wait there, with them, until the colonel should come and tell them what had been discovered at the museum about Mr. Hawthorne's death.

"It is no trouble," Mrs. Merriweather replied. "But I cannot think it likely the colonel and the Runner will discover anything of great importance today. Not unless someone was extraordinarily careless. And from what I saw at the museum, I think that most unlikely."

"Nonetheless, I shall wait," the captain said with quiet certainty.

Perhaps Lady Merriweather would have been more amiable, more welcoming at the sight of unexpected guests, if they had not arrived quite so unexpectedly or quite so early in the day.

"It is not even noon!" Lady Merriweather said in angry accents to Marian after she drew her aside, ostensibly to consult on the best room in which to put Miss Hawthorne. "What on earth do you mean bringing these strangers into my house and demanding that I house one of them?"

There was a great deal Marian was tempted to say to her hostess. Instead, she said what she needed to say in a way that Lady Merriweather might be inclined to view it in a favorable light. She explained to her the lineage of both Miss Hawthorne and Captain Stanfield and their connections, however slight, to some of the leading families of the *ton*. Granted, Miss Hawthorne had no surviving relatives, but her father's family had once been very much respected indeed.

Marian spoke so quickly that she left Lady Merriweather more than a little bewildered. She also left her with the sense that perhaps she ought not to offend such modestly attired young people who had such powerful, if unsuspected, connections. In any event, Lady Merriweather went from looking as if she were about to ring a peal over everyone's head for presumption, to looking as if she was grateful for Miss Hawthorne and Captain Stanfield's condescension in deigning to honor her home with their presence.

Marian only hoped the entire matter would be resolved before Lady Merriweather untangled all the details and discovered that if her nephew's wife had not precisely lied, she had at the very least enlarged upon certain details to the apparent benefit of the two young people. In any event, it bought them some much-needed time.

# 5

Colonel Merriweather paused in the doorway of the drawing room. He expected Marian to be there, of course, and his aunt, Lady Merriweather, but he was rather taken aback to see Miss Hawthorne and Captain Stanfield. He cleared his throat, and immediately all eyes turned to him.

He spoke first to Miss Hawthorne. "I am very sorry, my dear, about the loss of your father. He was a good man."

"Yes, he was," she answered in a voice that betrayed how close to the edge she was. "Have you learned anything about who might have killed him, or why?"

The colonel shook his head. "Thieves, perhaps. But that is only a guess, and we cannot know for certain until we catch the person. Collins, the Bow Street Runner, suggested it might have been Tom, but I told him I thought that most unlikely."

"Impossible!" Miss Hawthorne answered at once. "Tom adored my father. He would have done anything for him. My father, you see, is the only one who has always treated him with respect. Everyone makes fun of Tom because his understanding is not strong. But he is a kind and gentle soul and would never hurt anyone—certainly not my father!"

The colonel nodded. "So I told the Runner. Er, Marian, I should like to speak with you privately. Shall we walk in the garden?"

"Of course."

She came at once. It was one of the things the colonel liked best about his wife, that she possessed such common sense, such superior understanding. In point of fact, he often thought that her understanding might be almost as superior as his own.

He waited until they were outside; then he said with what he felt to be great patience, "My dear, why are Miss Hawthorne and Captain Stanfield here? I was very much taken aback when the Dearborns and I arrived at Hawthorne's home to discover that his daughter was not there. It is a very good thing I had already arranged for someone to stay with the body. But why is she here?"

Marian told him. She spoke succinctly, and in a few moments he understood.

"Good heavens!" he exclaimed. "Are you certain you are all right?"

"Yes, my dear," Marian said fondly. "But you can see why I could not leave Miss Hawthorne there. Not even if you were going to arrange to have someone at the house. I trust that Dearborn is capable of defending himself, if need be?"

The colonel nodded. "More than capable. Though I shall want to send round a note to warn the couple. And I will admit I think it wiser to have Miss Hawthorne stay with us. But what is Captain Stanfield doing here?"

Marian could not help but look rather pleased with herself. Still, her voice was as offhand as she could manage as she said, "Captain Stanfield accompanied us to Hawthorne's home. After what happened there, I suppose he wished to come here with us to make certain that nothing further went amiss. I could not make him see that it was unnecessary. He is either protective of Miss Hawthorne, or he wished to be here when you returned, to hear what you might have learned. But I rather think it is Miss Hawthorne's welfare that concerns him most."

The colonel listened with increasing agitation to this explanation. When she finished, he tried to choose words to show her the folly of interfering so in the life of a young man and woman she scarcely knew. But before he could do so, his wife spoke again.

"But enough of that! Tell me, my dear, what did you learn today that you didn't wish the others to know?"

He eyed her with some asperity. He wanted to give her a set down, but he knew she would simply keep interrupting him until he told her what she wished to know.

"Very well, Marian. The Runner wished, as I said inside, to accuse Tom. When I made it clear that was not the proper solution, he persevered. We found Hawthorne's office in complete disarray."

"Perhaps it is always so?" Mrs. Merriweather suggested. "Many scholars are not tidy people."

"You forget that I saw his office only yesterday. And it was untidy, but nothing like what we found today. No, someone must have searched it thoroughly."

"Truly? I wonder what they were looking for? They must not have found it, or there would have been no reason to go to his house."

"Now, now, Marian, do not become eager in such an unbecoming way! It is only a theory, after all."

"Yes, but you think it matters," Mrs. Merriweather pointed out shrewdly, not in the least daunted by his sensible reply. "Have you any notion who it could be? Someone from inside the museum, or outside? Did the porter say whether anyone had come in as early as Mr. Hawthorne? Did he mention, in particular, whether anyone who did not work at the museum came early?"

The colonel looked down at his feet. How the devil had they come to this? He had only meant to bring Marian out here to ask about those two young people. He wished he could simply tell her that this was none of her affair, but he knew her too well to believe she would accept such an answer. Fortunately, from the colonel's point of view, at any rate, his aunt chose that moment to interrupt them.

"Andrew! I am not pleased about the goings-on here

today," Lady Merriweather said, coming straight up to the pair of them. "Your wife simply appeared on my doorstep, before noon, and informed me that I am to house this Miss Hawthorne here! What could I do but agree? But I tell you now that I am not pleased, not pleased at all!"

"We could remove to a hotel," Mrs. Merriweather suggested with a hopeful gleam in her eye.

The colonel frowned at his wife. "Not now, Marian. Aunt Cordelia, I agree that you have been put upon outrageously. I am certain my wife would never have done so if she had not known so well your generous nature. And, in point of fact, you would be doing me a tremendous favor if you let the child stay. My work at the British Museum will be much easier if she is near at hand to talk with, since she worked so closely with her father, who is now dead. She may be the only one who can answer my questions about what must be done."

The colonel spoke in his most charming manner, a charm to which his aunt was indeed still susceptible. She tried to look stern, but after a moment she relented. "Oh, very well. The girl may stay." She paused and turned to the colonel's wife and said, "You ought to have told me straightaway that it was for Andrew's sake that you were asking."

Marian seemed to struggle with herself, but then she said in a surprisingly amiable voice, "I would have done so, Lady Merriweather, but how could I when I had represented to Miss Hawthorne that I was asking her here for her benefit? I could not tell you the truth without perhaps causing her to refuse to stay, and then what would Andrew have done?"

This last was said with a melting look at the colonel. He was not deceived. Marian was playacting again, and while he was, in this instance, grateful, he did not like it. She was up to something more than she had said, and he wasn't quite certain whether he ought to demand to know what it was, or whether his peace of mind would be better served if he didn't!

\*   \*   \*

Inside the house, Captain Stanfield moved his chair closer to Miss Hawthorne. "I have not had the chance to tell you how sorry I am about your father," he told her.

"You said all that was proper back at the museum," she replied stiffly.

William hesitated. "All that was proper, perhaps, but not everything that I felt. I am concerned for you, Miss Hawthorne. What will you do now?"

She shrugged. Unwillingly, it seemed to him, she unbent a trifle. Enough, at any rate to say, "For a while, I shall continue to go to the museum every day. And try to carry on my father's work. There is no one else to do so, so I shall do my best. At least until I am told I am no longer wanted there. I fear that shall not take very long. Few will think a woman capable of filling my father's shoes. But for as long as I can, I shall try."

"I see." William hesitated. He quite agreed with those who thought the museum was no place for a woman. But he could scarcely say so to Miss Hawthorne, or to Mrs. Merriweather, for that matter. Not when she considered herself capable of taking part in the investigation of a murder! But he had to say something, so he told Miss Hawthorne, "I shall, of course, continue to come to the museum and help as well."

She turned to him then, gratitude in her blue eyes that threatened to spill over with tears. "Thank you," she said, her voice scarcely louder than a whisper. "You and the colonel were such a help to my father, and I know he would be grateful that you did not simply abandon the work you have begun."

Now the tears did begin to spill down her cheeks, and without thinking how it would look, without worrying what might be proper, Captain Stanfield removed the spectacles from Miss Hawthorne's nose and drew her into his arms, where he cradled her head against his shoulder. He could feel her grief and was powerless to stop it. All he could do was hold her and murmur reassurances to the top of her head.

He also silently cursed himself for a fool. He wasn't supposed to get involved! He was supposed to be at the museum for a purpose, and that purpose had not changed with Mr. Hawthorne's death.

He ought not to feel this tug at his heartstrings, this odd desire in his breast to protect Miss Hawthorne. She ought to be nothing and no one to him. He was a solitary fellow. It had always been that way. Certainly he had never before had any desire to fall prey to a pretty face.

Not that one would say Miss Hawthorne had precisely a pretty face. It was more one that would be described as having character and intelligence. Perhaps that was what drew him to her. The fact that she was not at all like the society ladies his mother and sisters were constantly attempting to foist upon him. No, Miss Hawthorne was not conventionally pretty.

But here he was, holding Miss Hawthorne and oddly reluctant to let her go. Here he was, despite it being none of his affair, wishing he could ease her sorrow, smooth her way, and make certain that no one hurt her. But there was Mrs. Merriweather to do so, wasn't there? She certainly seemed competent in that regard. Surely he ought to simply step away? And yet, he could not.

At the same moment, both William and Miss Hawthorne heard footsteps in the hall. Hastily they moved apart, not wishing to make matters worse by being caught in such a scandalously close embrace. Somehow William did not think Lady Merriweather the sort to believe he had just been comforting Miss Hawthorne, and if she did not, she would make the young woman's stay in this house deucedly uncomfortable. Beside him, Ariel settled her spectacles back upon her nose.

It was not Lady Merriweather, however, who entered the drawing room, but rather Colonel and Mrs. Merriweather. He came straight to the point.

"Mrs. Merriweather has told me what happened," he said. "Are you all right, my dear?"

Ariel nodded.

"How fortunate that your father kept a pistol at home, Miss Hawthorne, and taught you how to use it," Mrs. Merriweather said approvingly.

"Here, now! Far better that Miss Hawthorne should not have needed such a thing in the first place," the colonel said with some alarm.

"To be sure, it would have been better if there had been no intruder," Mrs. Merriweather conceded soothingly. "But since there was one, I think it just as well that Miss Hawthorne had the means at hand to defend herself, should it have been necessary."

"I would have defended her if it had been necessary," Captain Stanfield protested indignantly.

Mrs. Merriweather smiled at him indulgently. "To be sure," she repeated. "Nonetheless, it is my experience that it is always wise if a lady can defend herself as well."

This was, however, more than the colonel wished to hear. He broke in to ask Miss Hawthorne, "Have you any notion what the man could have been after?"

She hesitated, then shook her head. "Papa had no money, and I cannot think anyone would break into the house for his research."

The colonel sighed. "Never mind, my dear. At least you are safe here. Marian, why don't you take Miss Hawthorne upstairs so that she may rest?"

Mrs. Merriweather regarded him oddly for a moment, then nodded and held out a hand to the younger woman, who took it without protest and let herself be led out of the room. The moment the ladies were gone and the two men alone in the room, the colonel regarded William with a shrewdness that was disconcerting.

The colonel smiled a wintry sort of smile and said, "Who the devil are you, m'boy?"

Stanfield made a choking sound. "Sir?" he asked warily.

The colonel gave a sigh of exasperation. "Do not trifle

with me, Captain Stanfield! I know you are not what you seem! Yes, yes, you served in the Peninsula. And yes, yes, Wellington did ask you to come and help Hawthorne sort through the artifacts. But why did he ask you? Who put him up to that, I wonder?"

Stanfield wished he could loosen his cravat, but that would only have betrayed him. Instead he took a deep breath and attempted to brazen it out. "I don't know what you mean, sir," he said. "It came as much as a surprise to me as it came to you that I was asked."

"I see. And you don't mean to tell me anything more? It's a mistake, m'boy. A mistake."

"May I ask why you are so certain I am not who I say I am?" Stanfield asked through gritted teeth.

"I didn't say you weren't who you say you are, only that you are more than you seem." The colonel took a chair opposite the younger man. "Take, for example, your injury. I know about injuries. Saw far too many of 'em in the war. Been asking a few friends about yours. Seem much surprised to hear you should still walk with a cane, still need to have your arm in a sling, after all these years."

"I fell from a horse," Stanfield said, feeling a sense of desperation, "not two months ago. That reopened the old injuries, which is why you see me this way now."

The colonel nodded. "Perhaps. But the odd thing is, I'm told you gave the same excuse when you were visiting up in the wilds of Yorkshire, a year ago. Do you make a habit of falling off horses?"

"I, er, that is to say—"

"No!" The colonel held up a hand to forestall him. "Tell me no more lies. The truth or nothing, m'boy."

Stanfield was silent. He neither confirmed nor denied the charges. After a long moment the colonel nodded again. "So that's the way of it. I'm very sorry, for I had hoped to help you. Now, I give you fair warning. If I find you've anything to do with the murder, or plan anything against the museum, I shall stop you. And I tell you right now that I shall do my best to protect Miss

Hawthorne from you. And should you offer any insult to Mrs. Merriweather, you will truly discover how awful my anger can be. Get out of this house at once!"

Stanfield rose to his feet. He had all but flinched under the colonel's verbal assault. Now he drew himself to his full height. "I am very sorry to have disappointed you, sir, and that you do not trust me. I had not wanted it to be this way."

The colonel snorted. "Pretty words, but they won't pay the toll."

Stanfield bowed. "Good day," he said, and left.

# 6

Deep in the museum, Tom tried to settle down for the night. He wasn't happy. Mr. Hawthorne had always been kind to him. Who would be kind now? Miss Hawthorne was kind. But she wouldn't be staying long. They wouldn't let her. He heard people talk, he did. And they talked about her. About Miss Hawthorne. Said she shouldn't be there. Her father brought her to the museum anyway. But now he was gone and they would say she should go. They would probably say he should go, too.

That scared Tom. Where would he go? Who would give him a place to stay? Mr. Hawthorne let him live here, in this room. Told him he could be the night watchman. But now he was dead. And that made Tom angry. Angry enough, when he heard the noises, to go see.

He didn't usually go to see about noises. Not since the night they told him to be quiet or he would get hurt. He didn't usually even wake up to hear the noises. But tonight he was too angry to care. Maybe they were the ones who had hurt Mr. Hawthorne. If they were, he was going to tell. He was going to tell Miss Hawthorne. He was going to tell Captain Stanfield. He was going to tell the colonel and his lady. He was going to tell everyone.

He opened the door to his room and followed the sounds. He tried to be quiet, Tom did. But right before he got to the room where they were talking, saying something about Mr. Hawthorne, he tripped over something.

He knew by the way they suddenly stopped talking that they had heard him. He turned to run, suddenly afraid. He'd only gone a few feet when the shot rang out. Tom felt something burning in his chest. It hurt! He reached out for the wall but fell to the floor anyway.

No! He had to tell!

Tom never told anyone anything ever again.


In another part of town, Stanfield read the message Thornsby had sent him. Now he knew who the colonel was and who his wife had been. Granted, he had already known who the colonel was, but not about his connections. Nor had he recognized Mrs. Merriweather, the former Miss Tibbles. But now he knew why she looked so familiar.

To be sure, he had only seen Miss Tibbles a few times, when he was a small boy. She was governess to a cousin of his. A wild hoyden of a girl, his cousin had been. The family still spoke of her in hushed accents. And about the miracle Miss Tibbles had wrought, teaching his cousin to behave with at least a semblance of propriety. She had, he recalled, married well and settled into a happy appearance, at least, of complacency with the rules of the *ton*. She was due to bring out her own daughter soon, and what an interesting time that would be.

William shook his head. He was allowing himself to be distracted. Except, perhaps not entirely. For the fact that Mrs. Merriweather was the former Miss Tibbles did matter. It meant that she was preternaturally alert and inclined to notice what one most hoped she would not. And that could present him with problems as he attempted to carry out Thornsby's instructions.

He rather wished he could confide in the colonel or the former Miss Tibbles. It would have been reassuring to have them as allies. But Thornsby's orders were explicit. For now, at any rate, no one must know the truth of what Stanfield was doing at the museum. No one must guess him to be more than the former soldier he appeared to be. Except, of course, that the colonel already had.

With a sigh, William wondered what Thornsby would make of the note he had sent back with the messenger. What he would say when he learned that someone had killed Hawthorne. Even more, however, he wondered what Miss Hawthorne was doing tonight. And whether, perhaps, she was thinking about him. If so, he wondered what she was thinking.

Ariel was, of course, thinking of Captain Stanfield. She kept remembering the way he had held her earlier when she needed to cry about Papa. She kept remembering the gentleness with which he had stroked her hair and wiped away the tear on her cheek. She was not accustomed to kindness. Not since Mama died. Papa had been a good man, and an even better scholar, but he had never understood about kindness.

Indeed, as Ariel leaned against the window ledge and stared out at the night sky, she found herself remembering more than just Captain Stanfield's kindness. She found herself remembering the way *she* had felt when his hands stroked her hair. She didn't understand it. It was something entirely unaccustomed for her, something Ariel had never felt before. Not even during the brief time she had been courted by the young scholar her father was once so fond of—before he discovered the fellow was trying to steal his research notes.

What flaw was it in her character, Ariel wondered, that the same day her father died she could wish for Stanfield to hold her and stroke her hair again? Could wish, indeed, for more scandalous things than that! Into her mind came the image of Captain Stanfield kissing her. She yearned for it more than she could say, and a wave of loneliness swept over her. Just as she turned to climb back into bed, there was a knock at her bedroom door.

Surprised, Ariel tried to compose herself as she went to see who could be so bold-faced as to disturb her at such an hour. It was, she discovered, Mrs. Merriweather.

"Hello, my dear," the older woman said in a kindly voice. "I wanted to make certain that you were all right."

"Y-yes, of course I am," Ariel replied.

Mrs. Merriweather stepped forward, into the room, and Ariel had little choice but to step back. "Are you?" the colonel's wife asked.

She ought to have answered calmly; she ought to have insisted that she was. But there was something about the somewhat short and slightly plump older woman that made one want to confide in her. And instead of sending Mrs. Merriweather away, Ariel found herself saying, in a voice that gave way as she did so, "No, I am not all right. I do not feel as if I shall ever be all right again!"

Mrs. Merriweather reached out and Ariel went into the arms she held wide open. And for the second time that day she gave way to tears. It was absurd, it was foolish, it was not at all what her papa would have said she should do, but it happened. Mrs. Merriweather, much like Captain Stanfield, held Ariel and stroked her hair and murmured soothing words while the younger woman cried.

When at last she had no more tears left, Ariel pulled away and Mrs. Merriweather made no effort to stop her. Instead she chose a chair and indicated that Ariel should sit in the one beside it.

"You feel lost, don't you?" she asked.

"Yes," Ariel replied warily.

Mrs. Merriweather met her gaze steadily. "You wonder how I know," she said. "It is because I was even younger than you when I lost my father. That is how I came to be a governess. My father died having lost everything, and I had no one to turn to. It was very, very hard."

She paused and took a deep breath. "Perhaps it is too soon to broach the subject," Mrs. Merriweather said, "but tonight I found myself thinking of you and wondering about your circumstances. I know that we ladies are not supposed to bother our heads about such matters, but that is nonsense when we are so deeply affected! And so I wished to ask you, my dear, whether you know upon what financial terms your father has left you. Will you have sufficient funds to meet your needs, or will you need to earn your way? Forgive me for prying, but I only ask because if it is so, perhaps I can help you."

Ariel hesitated. "I don't know," she said. "That is to say, we never seemed precisely pinched for funds, but neither were we ever flush in the pocket. I do not know how much of what we lived upon was Papa's salary at the museum and how much might have been an inheritance or something of that sort. So you see, I honestly do not know what my circumstances are or what I shall have to do. I should like to take over Papa's position, but of course that is not likely to happen. A woman would never be allowed to hold the post, no matter how well Papa taught me what he knew."

"I have no doubt you are right about the post at the museum," Mrs. Merriweather said in dry tones. "As for the rest, well, do you know the name of your father's solicitor? If so, then perhaps, after the funeral, we should go see him. We shall need to discover what, if any, inheritance there might be. Once that is known to us, we can begin to make plans for your future."

Ariel nodded. "I do know his name. Mr. Renfred. And while I do not very much feel like being practical right now, I suppose you are right that I must do so anyway."

Mrs. Merriweather nodded and patted the younger woman's hand. "I know. I remember how I felt. All I wished to do was crawl into bed and never come out. But it was not possible for me and it will not do for you. The situation must be faced. At least in your case, my dear, I can make certain you need not face it alone."

"It is more than that," Ariel said quietly. "I find myself thinking that I ought to be with my father's body. It seems a betrayal to be here instead, to be talking of solicitors and inheritances. I ought not to be thinking of whether I might benefit from his death."

"Why not?" Mrs. Merriweather asked shrewdly. "Are you afraid you will be angry if he made very little provision for you? Or simply guilty at the notion of thinking of anything besides his loss?"

"Both," Ariel said in a voice so low that Mrs. Merriweather had to strain to hear her.

"Oh, my dear!" the older woman said, placing her hand over Ariel's. "I truly think your father would have understood. He did not seem to me to be a man who cared overmuch for excessive mourning."

In spite of herself, in spite of her grief, Ariel smiled. "You are right," she agreed. "Papa had little patience for it. I still remember that the day after Mama died, he was at the museum, deep in work, and he took me with him. He said we must be practical. And I suppose he would say the same again, were he here now to advise me."

She took a deep breath and looked at Mrs. Merriweather. "I know that Papa would be impatient with me for crying over what he would have called his empty shell. I can almost hear his voice saying that the best way to show my respect for him is to carry on his work at the museum, so long as they will let me. He would tell me to take care of myself and to make myself useful. No, I need to mourn Papa, not for his sake but for my own."

Mrs. Merriweather nodded. "I understand," she said. "Tomorrow morning we shall go to the museum and you will do what you can to carry on your father's work. In the afternoon we shall go to your house to sit with your father's body for as long as you feel the need to be there. Will that do?"

Ariel did not trust herself to speak, and so she nodded instead. It helped so much to have someone who understood. As much as she loved him, Papa never had.

The older woman rose to her feet. Her voice was brisk

but soothing as she said, "I shall let you get some sleep now, though it may be hard to come by after the events of today. Still, you must try. And tomorrow, I promise you, we shall find a way to sort out your future."

And with that Mrs. Merriweather turned and left the room. Behind her, Ariel could only continue to sit, ensnared in the numbness that had held her captive all day. Frightened of the grief that she had been able to let herself feel only in the safety of Captain Stanfield or Mrs. Merriweather's company. Alone it felt too terrifying, too overwhelming, to even admit such grief existed.

But she could not stay in the chair all night. At some point she moved to the bed. Mrs. Merriweather's description of wishing to climb into bed and never come out, yes, that felt just right to Ariel. She wished she could do precisely that. But it was impossible. She had to go to the museum and work. All too soon, the trustees would tell her that she was no longer welcome there. She would also stop by the house and see that whomever the colonel had hired was treating her father's body with respect— shell or not, he deserved that much.

Thanks to Mrs. Merriweather, she need not face any of it alone. For that kindness, Ariel was profoundly grateful.

# 7

It was a somber group that met the next morning at the museum. None of them had managed a full night's sleep, and yet all of them, the colonel, Mrs. Merriweather, Captain Stanfield, and Miss Hawthorne, were determined to be there. They worked on sorting through the artifacts with unaccustomed quiet, barely speaking save when it was absolutely necessary. Hawthorne's death had cast a shadow over all of them.

Around midmorning, it became evident that they would need help moving one of the pieces, and Ariel offered to fetch Tom. "I shall go with you," Stanfield said at once.

Somewhat shyly, Ariel agreed. As they moved down the hallway, the captain leaned closer to her. "How do you go on, this morning?" he asked.

She met his gaze and answered honestly. "As well as might be expected. I miss my father very much, but I know he would want me to be here."

It was at that moment they turned the corner and saw something, or rather someone, slumped on the floor. They both moved more quickly, and suddenly Ariel realized what, or rather who, she was seeing. Her screams pealed through the halls of the museum and brought a crowd of scholars and clerks running, and of course Colonel and Mrs. Merriweather, as well.

The group clustered around the body, everyone speak-

ing at once. Ariel clung to Captain Stanfield. It didn't
seem possible, not two days in a row, to find people she
cared about had been killed. It was only his steady voice
speaking soothing words to her that kept Ariel from falling apart.

Someone sent for Mr. Collins, the Bow Street Runner.
He came and made copious notes. Then he announced
his conclusions. There was a stunned silence in the hallway after he did so.

"Killed Mr. Hawthorne, 'e did. Then couldn't take the
shame of it, so 'e killed 'mself."

"That's utter nonsense!" Mrs. Merriweather retorted
instantly.

"Tom would never have hurt Papa," Ariel protested.
"Nor would he have known how to load and use a gun,
even if he had had one."

"The gun is in 'is 'and."

There were murmurs of assent at this. It was felt to
be a valid point, at least by those not close enough to
see the actual body. Mrs. Merriweather, however, could
see the body and she did not think the point a valid one
at all.

"Tom could not possibly have fired the gun and had
the bullet strike him in such a way. Could he, my dear?"
Mrs. Merriweather persisted.

Mrs. Merriweather appealed to the colonel, as well she
might, for he had seen a great many gunshot wounds
during the war. To be sure, those injuries had been from
rifle shots, but even so, he, too, agreed that the injury
could not have been inflicted by Tom. But he was reluctant to say so aloud. Not with so many interested ears
about.

"We must be absolutely certain, Collins, as to who
killed Mr. Hawthorne," the colonel told the Bow Street
Runner. "The trustees of the museum will wish to know.
They have decided to pay your fee and will not be satisfied for you to simply speculate that it was this poor
young man here."

"Aye, p'rhaps so," the Runner reluctantly agreed. "But won't no one care about the cause of this 'ere feller's death, now will they?"

"They will if his death is tied to that of Mr. Hawthorne," Colonel Merriweather pointed out.

"If that's so and we catches Mr. 'awthorne's murderer, then we'll 'ave this feller's, too," Collins retorted, jutting out his chin defiantly. "No one is going to pay me for finding 'is murderer, so I ain't about to waste me time. The gun is in 'is 'and, so won't no one question us if we say the young man killed 'imself."

There were mutterings from the others, and the colonel and the Runner moved a small distance from the crowd to discuss the matter in a more private way.

Ariel looked at Mrs. Merriweather. Her face was very pale, and she looked as though she might faint. But she was stronger than she looked.

"I cannot believe, I will not believe, that Tom killed my father. Nor that he killed himself. It simply isn't possible," she repeated.

"I quite agree," Mrs. Merriweather said.

"Yes, well, we must hope the Runner can sort it all out," one of the museum staff said, coming to stand beside Ariel. "You should not stay here, Miss Hawthorne. You ladies should not be subject to such an appalling sight."

Mrs. Merriweather and Ariel both turned to stare at the young man in disbelief. "My dear sir," Mrs. Merriweather said, drawing herself up to her full diminutive height, "I have, I will assure you, been subject to far worse sights over the last twenty years. I have been kidnapped and bashed over the head and seen more than one dead body. This one will not send me into the vapors. But if the sight is too distressing to you, pray leave any time you choose."

Another staff member stepped forward. "That may be very well for you, whoever you are, ma'am," he said boldly, "but perhaps Miss Hawthorne would be glad of a respite from such an appalling sight. After all, she knew poor Tom. We all did."

The other staff members nodded in agreement. Ariel smiled wanly at them. "You are kind to worry," she said. "But I cannot simply walk away and leave Tom here."

Now it was Captain Stanfield who stepped in. "I share your concern about Miss Hawthorne," he told the staff members gathered around. "And I promise all of you that if it seems to be too much for her, I shall make certain she goes home and rests."

They did not want to agree; Ariel could read the doubt in their eyes. And she was touched by their concern. They had not wanted her here, invading their male sanctum, when her father first brought her in to help him with his work. But they had come to accept her, and now they worried over her as if she was someone they had truly come to care about.

"I cannot like it," the first one who had spoken persisted. "We worry about you, Miss Hawthorne."

"We all worry about Miss Hawthorne," Mrs. Merriweather said briskly. "But the captain and I are well able to take care of her."

"Who *are* you?" one of the staff members demanded with some exasperation.

"I am Mrs. Merriweather, Colonel Merriweather's wife. We were helping Mr. Hawthorne to catalog the items donated to the museum by the Duke of Wellington," she answered austerely. "I am also a former governess and therefore well schooled and well experienced in how to deal with a young lady overcome by intense emotion. Can you say the same?"

It was a telling reply. These were scholars and clerks. They could do little more than bow and retreat. And they did so, but not before the eldest one turned to Ariel and told her warmly, "If you need anything, Miss Hawthorne, anything at all, I pray you will let us know."

"Perhaps they are right," Stanfield said awkwardly after the staff members had left. "Perhaps this is too much for you to deal with, so soon after your father's death, Miss Hawthorne.''

"No!" Ariel's voice was adamant. She drew in a deep breath and tried to explain. "Tom has been a part of my life for the past several years. I cannot leave before I know if the Bow Street Runner will make an effort to find out who killed him."

And with that she marched over to where the Runner and Colonel Merriweather were still talking quietly. "What are you going to do about Tom?" she demanded.

Startled, the Runner looked at her. "Do? Why send for 'is body to be taken to Potter's Field, I reckon. 'e ain't got no fam'ly. So 'e told me yesterday.''

Ariel shook her head. "No. I will not have him buried in Potter's Field. He deserves better than that."

The Bow Street Runner looked at her with some exasperation. "Oh? And 'o'se to pay?" he demanded.

Ariel clenched her jaw. She wanted to say that she would, but she honestly did not know if her father had left her sufficient funds to do so. Mrs. Merriweather moved to her side. In a voice that was gentle, she asked, "If cost were not an issue, what would you wish to have done for Tom?"

"I would want Tom to be buried at the same time and in the same place as my father. It is what Papa would have wanted," Ariel replied. She paused and looked over at Tom's body. In a softer, wistful voice, she said, "We used to take Tom to church with us on Sunday mornings. He loved the music and seemed to find great comfort in it."

The colonel and Mrs. Merriweather exchanged looks. In the end, it was the colonel who gave way. "Yes, yes," he said. "I shall arrange for the body to be taken to your father's house, Miss Hawthorne. And I will see if it is possible for both men to be buried at the same time and in the same place." At a further look from Mrs. Merriweather he added, "And you needn't worry about the expense, either. Now, if you will excuse us, Collins and I have work to do. Marian, I suggest that you take

Miss Hawthorne home. Stanfield, do you care to assist Mr. Collins and myself?"

Ariel expected Mrs. Merriweather to argue with the colonel. But she did not do so. Instead she drew her lips together in a tight line, but all she said aloud was, "Yes, dear."

They watched until the men were out of sight. "Are we really going home?" Ariel asked.

Mrs. Merriweather hesitated. "I think perhaps it would be wise. We shall not be able to do any further work on the artifacts today anyway. It might be as well to go round to your house and find out what arrangements the couple my husband hired have made for your father's funeral. And see whether Tom may be buried then and there, as well."

Ariel looked at the older woman doubtfully. "The colonel said we were to go home."

"We shall," Mrs. Merriweather said with eyes wide open. "It is simply *your* home, not Lady Merriweather's, to which we shall go. If that was not what he meant, then he ought to have said so more clearly."

In spite of the layers of grief that threatened to overwhelm her, Ariel could not entirely choke back a small laugh at Mrs. Merriweather's reasoning. She glanced once more at Tom. It was true, she thought, that she could do nothing more for him here. And she was so very tired, after all.

Colonel Merriweather's carriage was waiting in the usual place. Once they were settled inside and on their way, Ariel said to Mrs. Merriweather, "If Tom was shot in the back, how could the Bow Street Runner possibly believe that he had killed himself?"

"He doesn't," Mrs. Merriweather replied tartly. "Mr. Collins knows very well that someone else must have shot Tom. But as you heard him say, he felt no one would pay him to prove such a thing, or to discover the murderer. And if he could have persuaded us that your father's murder was neatly resolved, he would have gotten his pay for that case and been done with his work.

The fellow, I fear, is a laggard. Someone must prove him wrong. Particularly as I suspect your father's death may, in some way, be tied to Tom's. Perhaps the colonel or Captain Stanfield will discover something useful."

Soon enough they were at Ariel's home. She stepped down from the carriage with some reluctance. Mrs. Merriweather patted her arm soothingly. "Seeing your father's body," she said, "will not make his death any more or less real."

"But it will feel more real," Ariel replied.

Mrs. Merriweather did not dispute the truth of that observation. Instead, she said, "The colonel tells me that you will like Mr. and Mrs. Dearborn. He said you will be able to tell them your wishes, with regard to your father's and Tom's funeral, and they will be able to arrange everything for you." She paused, then added more gently, "Come, my dear. It's best to get it over with."

Still, Ariel hesitated, and the words caught in her throat as she said, "Until now, it is as if I have been able to tell myself I had dreamed Papa's death. As if, in my heart, I could pretend that tomorrow I would wake up and he would be there."

"I know," Mrs. Merriweather said softly. "But you still must face the truth sometime."

Ariel took a deep breath and mounted the steps to her front door. Mrs. Dearborn let them in, and Ariel discovered that Colonel Merriweather was quite right in thinking she would like the couple. Mr. and Mrs. Dearborn were a kindly pair, and the man had a distinctly military bearing to his person. They fussed over Ariel, sitting her down, holding her hand when she went into the parlor to see her father's body, and handing her a cup of tea when she came out.

Mr. Dearborn cleared his throat. "I sent around a note to the parish church to let the rector know about your father's death. Colonel Merriweather thought that was where you would wish him buried. And there's been those what came to pay their respects. I told 'em all you was away, but no more'n that. I hope that were all right?"

Ariel nodded. "Thank you," she said, the depths of her emotion making it impossible to say anything more. "We shall need to send around another note to the rector. There is another body being brought here, another person who will need to be buried. He was a friend of ours, Tom was, and I thought that perhaps they could share a funeral."

That set the couple to clucking over her again. "The rector, he came around to the house," Mrs. Dearborn told Ariel. "He said he could settle the funeral for any day you wanted. The sooner the better, he thought, particularly with the spell of warm weather we've been having. I'm sure he'll be able to handle this other fellow as well."

Ariel nodded again. She tried to tell herself that none of this mattered. That it was not her father in the parlor, and it would not be Tom keeping him company in a short while. It was, it would be, only the shells of the two men she had once known. What did it matter what was done with that shell? Except, of course, that it did.

Mrs. Merriweather spoke now to the Dearborns. "Miss Hawthorne would be grateful if you could arrange it for as soon as possible. There is no one who needs to be notified, no family coming any distance after all."

"Of course we will," Mrs. Dearborn said soothingly.

"I'll go over to the church now," Mr. Dearborn said, and left his wife pouring Ariel another cup of tea.


In another part of town, Stanfield stared across the desk at Thornsby. "Two deaths," he said. "Two deaths in two days. I don't like it, and I'm worried there might be more."

"Any ideas yet?" Thornsby replied.

"Yes. I want to include the colonel."

Thornsby shook his head. "No. Not unless it becomes

absolutely necessary. I won't risk a careless word spoken by the wrong person at the wrong moment."

"I do not think Colonel Merriweather would make such a mistake," William countered.

"Perhaps not. But he has a wife, and if he tells her, she might. It's too great a risk."

For a long moment, the two men stared at each other, and then Stanfield gave way, but not gracefully. "Very well. But you do understand that it may not be possible to keep him from discovering the truth?"

"It is your job to do so," Thornsby told him flatly. He paused and frowned. "You've changed. Care to tell me how or why?"

Stanfield stared back. "Perhaps I've begun to wonder if this is enough, if this is really what I wish to do."

Thornsby nodded. "It happens. Usually sooner rather than later. Well, after this one is done, you can have as much time as you need to figure it out. But for now, until it *is* done, I want your full attention on your work. It's too dangerous if it isn't, and I should hate to see you caught because you were distracted."

William drew himself up to his full height then, and his voice was brisk as he replied, "Yes, sir."

"Good. And Stanfield?" His voice halted the younger man at the door. In what could have almost been mistaken for paternal tones, Thornsby said, "Have a care for your own safety, as well as the work at hand."

# 8

The day of her father's and Tom's funeral dawned gray and dreary. A perfect match to Ariel's lowered spirits. But she forced herself to swallow some tea and toast, knowing that it was going to be a very long day. As she did so, the sun began to peek out from behind the clouds. Ariel was not certain whether to be grateful or to feel angry that the weather was not showing a proper respect for her grief.

But that was sufficiently nonsensical to draw a tiny, wistful smile from her. How she would have adored hearing her father just once more telling her what a foolish creature she was! It still seemed impossible that Papa was dead. Each time she went to the house, it was a shock to see his body lying there so still and lifeless. It was as if, as much as her mind knew he was gone, a part of her heart still hoped it was all a mistake, and that the next time she went to see him, he would suddenly sit up and chide her laughingly for having been foolish enough to believe he was dead. It was no easier to believe that Tom was dead, either.

With a sigh, Ariel set aside the breakfast tray the maid had been kind enough to bring her, Mrs. Merriweather having understood that she would not wish to come downstairs on this morning of all mornings. Now she rose to dress, and the maid waited to help her.

"It's a beautiful black silk, it is," the woman said respectfully.

Ariel nodded, not trusting herself to speak. The dress had been her mother's and she had altered it to fit herself. It was the only black dress she owned, because Papa had not ever wished her to wear mourning, not for anyone. Barbaric, he had called it. But in doing so he had ignored the knowledge he so highly prized. The knowledge that in every culture there were traditions to help one through times of grief, and that the very universality of such traditions argued for both their necessity and their efficacy.

On every other day, Ariel would honor her father's wishes, but today, on the day he and Tom were to be buried, Ariel would honor them both by wearing the black her father so despised. Because in her heart Ariel knew it would matter to her.

She stood still, unnaturally so, as the maid did up the hooks and eyes of her dress. Nor did she move as the maid dressed her hair and settled a black bonnet on her head and handed her gloves to wear.

"They will be waiting for you downstairs by now," the maid said softly, respectfully, when she was done.

Ariel nodded. Her own voice was soft and gentle as she replied, "Thank you. I do not know what I would have done without your help this morning."

The young woman flushed with pleasure, curtsied, and held the door open. Ariel took a deep breath, then went out of the room and down the stairs to where, indeed, Colonel and Mrs. Merriweather, and even Captain Stanfield were waiting for her. The stairs seemed endless, and the time it took to descend forever, but at last she stood among them and could see the approval in their eyes. They understood, even if her father would not have done so, why she needed to wear full mourning today.

Without another word, the front door was opened and Ariel was gently shepherded down the steps and to the waiting carriage. She found herself seated beside Captain Stanfield, and more than once she felt his troubled eyes upon her face. Opposite, Mrs. Merriweather also regarded her with more than a little concern. So much so that Ariel found herself wishing to cry out that she was not made of porcelain and would not shatter. But her manners were too good for that and so she stayed silent on the ride to the church.

Her father's and Tom's coffins were already there. The service was mercifully short. Her father had given short shrift to religion, calling it rampant superstition, but today, as it often had before, it brought Ariel comfort. Then it was time for the bodies to be taken to the grave site.

"Come, my dear. The colonel and Captain Stanfield will accompany your father and Tom to their final resting places. We shall go to your house where arrangements have been made to provide some refreshments, in the event there are some who wish to call upon you to extend their sympathies."

But Ariel pulled her arm free of Mrs. Merriweather's gentle grip. "No!" she said, "I wish to, I must, go with Papa and Tom to see them laid to rest!"

"But my dear, it is not done!" Mrs. Merriweather protested.

"Not done at all," the colonel concurred. "Go along with m'wife, Miss Hawthorne."

Ariel continued to back away from them, shaking her head. "No, I will, I must, at the least, go with my father's body. I don't care what is or is not done! He would want me there and I wish to be there."

The colonel started to argue again, but Captain Stanfield forestalled him. "No," he said quietly. "Miss Hawthorne shall do as she chooses. I shall escort her, if she wishes, and see that she is never alone."

Ariel felt tears trembling at the corners of her eyes, and she wiped them away with the back of her gloved hand. Her voice trembled as she replied, "Thank you, Captain Stanfield."

He only bowed and held out an arm to her. The colonel and Mrs. Merriweather looked at each other doubtfully, but ceased to argue. Instead they hastily conferred in whispers, and then Mrs. Merriweather went off to the waiting carriage to, as the colonel explained, oversee matters at the Hawthorne household. Ariel, Captain Stanfield, and Colonel Merriweather took their places with the other mourners behind the two caskets and followed the funeral procession to the cemetery.

Ariel scarcely noticed what was said or who was there. What mattered was that she was there to see her father's casket laid in the ground, and then Tom's. She was conscious that Captain Stanfield stood guard by her side. He alone seemed to understand her need to be there, and for that she was profoundly grateful to him.

Whispers around and behind her, warned Ariel that the news of her unorthodox behavior would be all over London by the morrow. But she did not care. What was gossip to her, who had never moved in fashionable circles anyway? What was gossip to her who never would?

Tears ran down Ariel's cheeks, unnoticed by her but not by Captain Stanfield. He pressed his own handkerchief into her hands and she was grateful, for it was of far more use than her own tiny scrap of one made of lace.

A number of the men tried to speak to her, but the apparent unorthodoxy of her presence at the grave sites seemed to render them all but inarticulate. Ariel wished them all to the devil, but she managed to be civil anyway. Still, she was grateful when she and Captain Stanfield finally stood alone beside her father's grave again, even Colonel Merriweather having retreated a short distance away to give them privacy.

And then Ariel began to talk, the words tumbling out. All the things she had been unable to say these past few days.

"I miss him so much, already! How shall I ever bear having him gone? How shall I go on without him? What am I to do without him to turn to? Why? Why did he have to die? And in such a horrible way?"

Captain Stanfield was silent, letting Ariel go on until the words slowly sputtered to a stop and she turned to him and stared wordlessly into his face, grief plain upon her face. Then, and only then, did he take her hand and speak.

"You will go on because you must. You will go on because it is what your father would have wished you to do," Stanfield said with great gentleness. "You will learn to study on your own. You will find your own path to what you are meant to do. You will never cease to miss your father, but you will learn to bear the pain. And you will find, I think, that you need not bear it alone."

Ariel stared up at him, desperately wanting to believe that his words were true. But before she could press him to say that he knew they were, Colonel Merriweather moved closer and cleared his throat ostentatiously.

"We had best be going," he said. "Mrs. Merriweather will be expecting us, and by now there will be those who have come to pay their respects to you, Miss Hawthorne. You ought to be there."

Ariel nodded, and with a visible effort she drew herself together. "Yes, of course you are right. Let us be going. I will need to thank my father's friends who care enough to come and say good-bye."

# 9

The next morning Ariel rose, ready to go to work again.

"My dear, you must be joking," Colonel Merriweather protested.

"You are going to the museum, aren't you?" Ariel asked.

"Well, yes, but it is not *my* father who died."

"Papa would have wanted me to go," she replied, undeterred.

"Perhaps it would be best if Ariel kept busy," Mrs. Merriweather pointed out to the colonel. "You must admit that it is the sort of thing he would tell her she ought to do, if he were here."

Reluctantly, the colonel conceded the point. Captain Stanfield, when he saw Ariel, was just as vocal in his objections, with no more success than the colonel had had. And yet, when she saw the room with all the artifacts, she found she could not stay there.

"I shall go and speak to Papa's colleagues," Ariel said, her voice thick with emotion.

"I shall go with you," Mrs. Merriweather said with sympathy.

"But who will take notes if you both go?" Colonel Merriweather demanded indignantly.

"You could, my dear," Mrs. Merriweather replied.

As he started to sputter, Ariel said soothingly, "I shall ask one of the clerks to come help you, sir."

He grumbled but allowed that it would be a tolerable

solution. Together Ariel and Mrs. Merriweather left the room. When they were alone, the former governess said, "I am glad you wish to speak with your father's colleagues. I have some questions I should like to ask of them."

"Questions?" Ariel echoed uncertainly.

Mrs. Merriweather nodded briskly. "Questions," she confirmed. "The colonel does not like me to investigate, but I wish to find out, if I can, what happened to Tom. To your father as well, but the Bow Street Runner, Mr. Collins, is already trying to find the answers to his death. No one, on the other hand, seems to care very much what happened to Tom. But I do."

"Why?"

"Because no one seems to care about Tom. No one seems to think his life of any great value. And that makes me angry. Because for so many years of my life, when I was a mere governess, far too many people would have said just the same about mine."

Ariel smiled. Indeed, she grinned in a most impertinent manner. "I cannot think, Mrs. Merriweather, that you have ever been a *mere* anything! I daresay you terrorized your charges, brought them straightaway into pattern cards of propriety, and generally managed everyone's life precisely as it ought to have been managed. And I would strongly suspect that you were considered invaluable to every family in whose home you stayed."

Mrs. Merriweather seemed more pleased than otherwise at these words, but she shook her head and said grimly, "I wish it were so, but it was not. Oh, I will allow that I was indeed a formidable presence. And I did succeed with every girl whose care and education I undertook. But valued? Not by most of the *ton*. Just as you and your father considered Tom invaluable, and yet he is considered unimportant by almost everyone else. So, too, was it for me."

"Well I value you, and so does the colonel, and so, I daresay would my father, if he were here to see what you were about," Ariel replied stoutly. "But I take your point, and I will do everything I can to help you. But how are we to learn what happened to Tom, if even the Bow Street Runner and the colonel cannot do so?"

Mrs. Merriweather frowned. "That I cannot yet answer. All we can do is keep our wits about us as we look around and speak to anyone who might have been about. Was there anyone who rightfully would have been in the museum the night Tom was killed?"

"Only Tom. There is a porter, but he would be outside, not in the museum itself."

"Who, besides your father and you would have been first to arrive in the morning?"

Ariel rattled off several names. Mrs. Merriweather nodded briskly. "Very well, let us go talk with them and see what, if anything, we may learn, either about Tom or about that morning. Perhaps someone saw something they do not even realize is important. Now, where do we find these people?"

"This way."

They found everyone easily enough. Unfortunately, none of the scholars or their assistants would admit to having seen anything out of the ordinary, either the morning of Mr. Hawthorne's death or the next morning when Tom's body was discovered. Except, of course, for the colonel and the Bow Street Runner moving about the museum and asking the most impertinent of questions. Indeed, they seemed rather annoyed at having their work interrupted yet again, and Ariel and Mrs. Merriweather wisely chose to gracefully retreat before anyone started to wonder why the two women were so curious.

"What do we do now? Go back to the hall and help the colonel?" Ariel asked.

"No," Mrs. Merriweather replied decisively. "I should like to go look again at the place where Tom was killed."

"Why?"

"I'll explain when we get there."

True to her word, Mrs. Merriweather conferred with Ariel as to precisely how Tom's body had fallen and then said, "I believe Tom must have been running that way,

which means, since I believe him to have been shot in
the back, that the person with the pistol must have been
firing from this direction. Let us see what we find if we
look into the rooms along the way."

Ariel made no objection. If Mrs. Merriweather believed she could find something useful in solving Tom's
death, she was more than content to help her. Tom had
been a kind and gentle, albeit simple, soul, and she
missed him.

Indeed, it was Ariel who noticed that something was
wrong in the third storage room on the right. At first it
was only a nebulous feeling, but gradually she realized
what it was that was disturbing her.

"Someone has been in here," she told Mrs. Merriweather, "and rearranged a number of boxes against
the wall."

"How do you know?"

"My father and I were in this room less than two
weeks ago. He was looking for something important,
something he feared had been misplaced."

"Did he find it?"

Ariel shook her head. "No. But I remember how particular Papa was to have everything up on the shelves just so.
And how he commented that he supposed it didn't matter
since we were the only ones who ever came in here, but
that it mattered to him nonetheless. I laughed at him at
the time, but it doesn't seem very funny right now."

Mrs. Merriweather patted her shoulder. "No, it
wouldn't," she agreed sympathetically. "Very well, do
not touch anything, nor even go any further into the
room, but tell me what else you may be able to notice."

For some moments, Ariel bent to the task, quite literally stooping down to study the floor as well as standing
on tiptoe to see as high as she could. Finally she turned
to Mrs. Merriweather, a troubled look upon her face.

"It may be simply my imagination," she warned the
older woman.

Mrs. Merriweather nodded. "Perhaps. But I should
like to hear your thoughts anyway."

Ariel spoke slowly, choosing her words with great care. "I remember that the floor was very dirty in here. I said something of the sort to Papa, that we ought to have Tom sweep, but Papa said the things in this room were very valuable. He did not wish to risk anything happening to any of them and would rather have a dirty floor than let anyone but ourselves into the room. I also remember that he locked the door as we left. He always kept it locked."

"But it is not locked this morning," Mrs. Merriweather said slowly. "And the floor, at least in the middle, shows a jumble of footprints. So a number of people, or one very active person, was in this room since that day you were in here with your father."

"I wonder if that is what Tom saw, and the reason he was killed," Ariel said softly.

Mrs. Merriweather nodded. "I should think it quite possible. Just what is—or perhaps I should say what was—in this room, Miss Hawthorne?"

"This was the room Papa kept the things from Egypt that were brought back almost twenty years ago. Papa put some of the things on display, but of course there isn't room for everything to be out. And the most valuable smaller pieces are kept in here. If a scholar wished to study these objects, Papa would give him a small room in which to do so and bring them to the person one by one. He was so careful, you see, because at one time there was so much desire for Egyptian things that one or two objects were actually taken from the main rooms where they were on display."

Mrs. Merriweather drew in her breath in dismay. "Yes, I remember when all the most fashionable ladies were having their drawing rooms done up in Egyptian themes," she said slowly. "And I am not certain it has ever gone entirely out of fashion. I would not be surprised to discover that Tom interrupted the theft of objects from this room. Very well, since we have sorted out everything we can sort out simply by standing here, we may as well actually go into this room and examine the objects that are here!"

Ariel agreed. She moved briskly to the far side of the room and began to lift down boxes. Several times she frowned, uncertain. Eventually she got to the one that held her father's special treasure. It wasn't the most famous piece. The Rosetta Stone was the best known and most important one. But this was her father's personal favorite. It was a small statue of a cat that he kept in a wooden box on the shelf. The box didn't feel empty, but the moment Ariel lifted the lid she gave a cry of dismay.

Instantly Mrs. Merriweather was at her side. "What is it, my dear?"

Ariel lifted the statue out of the box. "This isn't right," she said with a frown. "It looks almost right. And if one didn't know it so well, one would never guess. But Papa used to take this piece out often and show it to me. There was a small imperfection near the paw that this piece does not have. Someone has made a careful copy, but missed that detail."

Mrs. Merriweather nodded. Her expression was grim as she said, "I can well imagine this would be worth a great deal—or rather the original would have been. I wonder if someone would have considered it worth committing murder for."

"But if someone wished to steal something," Ariel said slowly, "why would they take this piece and not something like the Rosetta Stone, which is far more valuable?"

"Precisely because the Rosetta Stone is so well known, one would not wish to risk being caught with it," Mrs. Merriweather suggested. "In any event, if one wished an object simply to look at, I would think this small statue of a cat would be more desirable. After all, it was your father's personal favorite for just that reason, I presume."

Ariel nodded. "So it was."

"Put it back, my dear," Mrs. Merriweather said briskly.

"Put it back?"

Mrs. Merriweather smiled at the note of incredulity in Ariel's voice. "Yes, put it back. And when we leave this room you are going to lock it up. You do have a set of keys, do you not?"

Ariel flushed. "I am not supposed to have keys," she said.

"But you do, don't you?"

"Yes."

"Good. Then you may lock the room. I do not, however, believe we need inform any of the gentlemen, or the Bow Street Runner, that you possess a set of keys. It will be far more handy if they do not know or guess."

Ariel found this view of matters most interesting and made not the slightest objection to Mrs. Merriweather's plans. She did as the older woman told her, and a few minutes later they were back in the corridor outside the room, the door securely locked against further intrusion.

"Though we must assume," Mrs. Merriweather said thoughtfully, "that whoever was in this room also has a set of keys. One wonders how many such sets there may be in existence, and who has hold of them."

Ariel might have tried to speculate, but at that moment, one of the men who worked at the museum rounded the corner and spotted them there. He seemed rather taken aback to find them there.

"Miss Hawthorne! What are you doing here? We thought you had gone home."

"Yes, yes, quite right, so she should, and so I have been telling her," Mrs. Merriweather said brightly. "We are looking for my husband. Colonel Merriweather. Have you perhaps seen him? It is such a warren of corridors and rooms here that we became quite turned around and lost. But now that you are here, you can show us the way to the room where Colonel Merriweather and Captain Stanfield are working."

If the young man thought it odd that Miss Hawthorne could have gotten lost in a place she had known most of her life, he did not say so. Perhaps he was distracted

by the very beguiling smile bestowed upon him by Mrs.
Merriweather. Or perhaps he chalked it up to grief. At
any rate, he did not ask any further questions. Instead
he led them, as requested, to the hall with the artifacts
Wellington had donated.

It was quite a tempting thought to Ariel to point out
that he was not taking them by the most direct route.
But then, he was one of the newer members to Papa's
staff so perhaps he had not yet learned his way about.
In any event, to have said anything aloud would have
put paid to Mrs. Merriweather's tale of the two of them
getting lost in the building. So she merely followed silently and mulled over what she and Mrs. Merriweather
had found. The young man left them the moment he had
directed them into the correct room.

"There you are," Colonel Merriweather said, with relief when he saw them.

"We were quite worried when we realized that both of
you were nowhere to be found," Captain Stanfield added,
coming forward as quickly as his injured leg would allow.

Stanfield spoke the words to both ladies, but his eyes
were on Ariel. And she felt herself grow warm under his
intense scrutiny. Was it possible, remotely possible, that
he, in some small way, cared what happened to her?

It was a thought she had not allowed herself to have
before, but now it seemed to crowd out all other possibilities. Until, that is, Mrs. Merriweather's brisk voice recalled her to her senses.

"I believe that Miss Hawthorne and I have, perhaps,
had quite enough excitement for today. We shall see you
back at Lady Merriweather's house later, Andrew."

Ariel would have protested, but a sharp glance from
the former governess stopped her. And, to be sure, she
was curious as to what the woman planned for them to
do next. She was fairly certain it was nothing so tame as
simply going straight back to Lady Merriweather's house.
She was quite right.

"Shall I accompany you ladies home?" Captain Stanfield asked.

"Oh, no, that will not be necessary," Mrs. Merriweather said brightly.

The colonel frowned. "It might not be a bad notion," he said. He paused and peered shrewdly at his wife. "You *do* mean to go straight home, don't you?" he demanded.

"I, er, thought I ought to take Miss Hawthorne shopping," Mrs. Merriweather said.

"Shopping?" both men echoed incredulously.

Mrs. Merriweather sighed. "Do none of you have any sense of propriety? Miss Hawthorne has lost her father. Do you not think it would be proper for her to wear some sort of mourning garb other than the one black gown she owns? It is imperative we find her something to signify that she has lost someone dear to her. Now do you still wish to accompany us?"

The men quite literally, rather comically and very hastily backed away. "No, no, that is quite all right. We would not wish to intrude."

Mrs. Merriweather wasted no further time but took Ariel's hand and led her to the entrance of the museum where the colonel's carriage was waiting, the coachman lounging very much at his ease. Mrs. Merriweather gave the fellow directions and bustled the younger woman inside.

Only when the carriage was on its way did Ariel have a chance to speak. "Papa did not believe in wearing mourning clothes," she said firmly.

"Good. Then we need not bother with a mantua maker," Mrs. Merriweather said briskly. "An arm band or some such thing will suffice. Your clothes are sober enough to satisfy. But with that tale, we have managed to escape the company of my husband and Captain Stanfield so that we may visit your father's solicitor on our own. I was able to discover Mr. Renfred's direction from Lady Merriweather's majordomo before we left the house this morning."

Ariel leaned back against the squabs. "You think of everything," she said.

"I try," Mrs. Merriweather agreed with a sniff of satisfaction. "I try."

Soon enough they were being shown into the solicitor's office. The clerk had tried to fob them off with a tale that Mr. Renfred was too busy to see them, but Mrs. Merriweather, who had tamed wild daughters and faced down earls and other peers in her day, had no trouble riding roughshod over the poor fellow so that he had no choice but to show them in at once.

Mr. Renfred was made of both sterner and shrewder stuff than his clerk. He took Mrs. Merriweather's measure in one glance and did not even attempt to distract her from her goal.

"I heard about your father's death, Miss Hawthorne, and meant to call upon you in a few days," he said when he had seen them both seated. "I presume you will wish to know in what position you stand with regard to financial matters."

Ariel nodded. "Papa never discussed money with me, and I have no idea whether he left me a pauper or not."

Mr. Renfred's gaze softened, and he removed his spectacles to polish them. When he put them back on his nose he said with proper gravity, "I am very sorry to hear of your father's death, Miss Hawthorne. He was a good man as well as a very clever one. Clever with money, I mean, and that is a fortunate circumstance for you. Your father left you well provided for. You will have three thousand pounds a year, which will provide you with quite a nice dowry, I should say."

"Three thousand pounds? A year?" Ariel blinked at the solicitor in disbelief. She turned to Mrs. Merriweather, as though instinctively feeling she might be better able to answer her next question than the solicitor. "But if Papa had so large a fortune, why did he insist that we live as we did?"

Mrs. Merriweather shook her head. "That I cannot answer, my dear. I must suppose his concern was to provide for the future. Or he had some purpose to which he meant someday to put those funds. I am afraid we shall never know, now that he is dead and we cannot ask him."

"I can tell you," the solicitor said, polishing his spectacles yet again. "Your father came into a small amount of money and asked me to invest it for him. He planned, Miss Hawthorne, to take whatever gains there were and travel to Egypt, after you were safely wed. Or so he told me. It is a great pity that he died without knowing that his investments have prospered far beyond any expectations he or I had for them, for I did not have a chance to tell him. And now I shall never be able to do so, nor shall he be able to take that trip that apparently mattered so much to him. But you, Miss Hawthorne, will benefit from his good fortune. You will never need to worry about finding yourself destitute, as too many ladies sometimes do."

In something of a daze, Ariel rose to her feet. "Thank you," she said, and started for the door.

The solicitor's voice stopped her. "I know you must be overwhelmed right now, Miss Hawthorne," he said kindly. "But I pray you will allow me to advance you some funds, until arrangements can be made for a steady allowance to be paid out to you. You need only let me know what you wish it to be, and I shall arrange everything."

Ariel waited while the solicitor fetched funds set aside, he assured her, for just such a purpose as this. She left his office with quite a large sum tucked into her shabby reticule, but she felt more overwhelmed than ever.

Beside her, Mrs. Merriweather said, in her brisk, practical voice, "I think, my dear, that we had best go shopping after all."

# 10

~~~

Ariel did not recognize herself in the looking glass Madame Salvage kept for the use of her customers. Papa had said he did not want her to wear mourning when he died, so the dress she was trying on was dark blue, rather than black. But it was of a finer fabric than she had ever worn before, and the cut far more flattering than any of the gowns she had made for herself over the years. There was a tiny place in her heart that was angry Papa had never let her know such a wonderful feeling before, while he was still alive.

When she had believed they could not afford for her to patronize a mantua maker, it had not mattered to Ariel. She understood and had never plagued her father over the fact. But it mattered now.

Mrs. Merriweather seemed just as pleased as Ariel with what she saw. She nodded approvingly to the mantua maker and said, in a matter-of-fact tone, "I believe Miss Hawthorne may wish to order a number of gowns from you, Madame Salvage, if you can provide some today and promise the rest of them quickly. And, of course, six months hence, she will need quite a few more brightly colored gowns. To that end, I wonder if you might be willing to perhaps adjust the price?"

Ariel drew in her breath in shock at Mrs. Merriweather's audacity. But apparently it was not as shocking as it seemed, for Madame Salvage agreed with great alacrity to the suggestion and soon the two women were deep in discussion of just how much could be done with the cost of all the gowns Mrs. Merriweather thought she ought to order.

Ariel supposed she should put a stop to this extravagance. She supposed she ought to insist she did not need more than one or two. But the fabric felt so soft against her skin, and the way she looked in the mirror was so appealing, that she could not summon up the strength of character to refuse the rest of the gowns. Not when it meant she could toss away all her older, unflattering clothing and look like this every day from here on out.

Besides, she soothed herself, from what Mr. Renfred had said today, Ariel could afford such extravagance—at least this once. And so she allowed herself to be persuaded. It was a very self-satisfied Mrs. Merriweather, and a tremulous Ariel, who left the now very happy Madame Salvage's establishment a short time later. Nor did it hurt that even Lady Merriweather, when shown Ariel's new finery when it arrived at the house a short time after they did, unbent sufficiently to bestow a more approving smile upon her than anything she had yet shown her thus far. If clothing could make such a difference, Ariel found she was glad she had let her objections be overcome!

Mrs. Merriweather had distressingly perceptive eyes. She watched Ariel, and when there was a quiet moment, drew her aside for, as she put it, a comfortable coze.

"What do you mean to do with yourself, now that you know you need not worry about funds?" Mrs. Merriweather asked.

It ought to have been an impertinent question, but Ariel understood the kindness in the other woman's voice and in her eyes. In any event, it was the same question she had been asking herself, ever since her father died. What would she do?

"I think, Mrs. Merriweather, that my plans have not changed such a great deal," Ariel said. "I shall continue to help sort out the artifacts at the museum until someone tells me that I must cease doing so. And then, well, then perhaps I shall travel a bit. Or find a snug little house somewhere where I may be comfortable."

The older woman nodded. She was silent for several moments before she said, choosing her words with great care, "Do you mean to travel alone? Live alone?"

Ariel gave a bitter laugh. "I know very well what society would say if I did so! So perhaps I will hire someone to travel with me, and when I return to live with me. I have the funds to do so now. Or perhaps I shall not care. It is not as if, after all, I expect ever to marry."

"Why not?"

"Why not?" Ariel echoed. "Look at me! I am not the sort of woman men wish to wed. I can think of only one man over the years who wished to do so, and in point of fact he merely wished to obtain Papa's trust so that he could steal my father's research! No, I do not think of marriage, Mrs. Merriweather, and it is not a kindness in you to remind me of that fact."

The older woman hesitated, and Ariel feared she had offended her. She ought to have known better. When Mrs. Merriweather did finally speak she said, "I have a strong notion you will not find yourself in such a position in the future. Indeed, I would guess that you may find yourself with a number of gentlemen wishing to make your acquaintance."

"Yes, drawn by the knowledge of the inheritance from my father!" Ariel retorted angrily. "I want no part of it, if the men are fortune hunters."

Now Mrs. Merriweather smiled, and there was a surprising hint of mischief in her eyes as she said, "Oh, I do not think they will all be drawn by your fortune. You are quite lovely now that you have a properly made gown."

The notion frightened Ariel. Gentlemen? Drawn to her? And drawn to her because she was lovely? What would she do if they were? What would she say? Nothing in her life had prepared Ariel for anything save the scholarly work she had helped her father to accomplish. No one had ever taken the time to try to teach her how to be a lady. Not since Mama died, and that was years ago.

As though she guessed the fear, Mrs. Merriweather leaned forward and put a hand over Ariel's. "Don't be afraid, my dear. It is actually rather pleasant to have a man say nice things to one. It is even rather pleasant to be a wife and mother."

"Papa said it wouldn't be," Ariel answered before she could stop herself. "Oh, later, when he had a scholar to whom he wished to pair me off, he said otherwise. But when I asked him for a Season, he told me I would hate such nonsense, that I would hate being a wife and mother. He told me all the disadvantages, you see, and I never forgot them, not even later when he wished to see me marry his protégé."

"I have no doubt it served his interests to say such things to you and have you believe them," Mrs. Merriweather replied in a dry voice. "Nor will I deny that marriage to the wrong man can be a horrible fate. But I would suspect your father's words came more out of his desire to continue to have you as a companion, an assistant, and so forth, than anything else. As with most things in life, you will find that marriage is very much what you choose to make of it. And a good marriage can be quite wonderful, I assure you."

Ariel regarded the other woman with a doubtful look in her eyes, but there was no mistaking the certainty with which Mrs. Merriweather spoke. Perhaps Papa had been mistaken. She would not think his motives any worse than that! Still, what did it matter what he had said?

She tilted up her chin in an unconscious gesture of defiance before she replied, "That is all very well, but I still do not expect to find anyone to marry."

"Why not? Have you never dreamed of having someone hold you close and comfort you when you are unhappy? Never dreamed of someone with whom to share your laughter? Never thought to hold your own child upon your lap?"

Ariel looked away. "Of course I have dreamed of such things. Who has not? But—"

"But you still have difficulty believing that it could ever happen to you?" Mrs. Merriweather suggested gently. Ariel nodded and the other woman smiled. "Perhaps it is time to try," she said.

Could she? It was a tempting thought, a very tempting thought. And Ariel did want to believe it was possible. Of course, it was most disconcerting that when she did begin to allow herself to imagine someday having someone love her, she saw the face of a certain former soldier who walked with a cane and had his arm in a sling. It was his eyes she found herself wanting to have regard her with warmth and affection and perhaps even approval. But that was foolish! Foolish beyond permission—wasn't it?

Ariel certainly could not allow herself to ask that question aloud! Instead she took a deep breath and forced herself to smile and say brightly, "I shall try, Mrs. Merriweather. But I still think it a most unlikely thing to ever happen to me."

Mrs. Merriweather patted Ariel's knee briskly, then said, "We shall know in time. But for now, we had best go and change for dinner. The colonel is waiting for me."

This last was said with a wink, and Ariel felt herself go warm at the thought of the colonel and his wife greeting each other with a kiss or embrace, certainly with the affection that seemed to visibly link them together. Would she ever have that in her own life? It was, she found, something she desperately wished she could.

Ariel was quite right. The colonel did greet his wife with both a kiss and a warm embrace. He also told her how much he approved of the transformation in Miss Hawthorne.

"Astonishing, m'dear, positively astonishing! I should never have guessed she could be such a taking thing. But can she afford new clothes such as these? The dress she is wearing looks quite expensive."

"It is expensive," Mrs. Merriweather agreed calmly. "And yes, Miss Hawthorne can afford as many such gowns as she wishes. So long as she is not entirely foolish, that is. It appears that Mr. Hawthorne left her very well provided for. Much more so than one would have expected from how he treated her while he was alive."

"And precisely how do you know this?" the colonel asked, bending a stern look upon his wife. "Have you been prying into her affairs? Surely she must have thought it impertinent of you to ask."

"I didn't ask," Mrs. Merriweather replied blithely. "Or, rather, I did, but Miss Hawthorne didn't know in what circumstances her father had left her. So I helped her discover the direction of her father's solicitor and we visited him today and he gave us the gratifying news."

"Marian!"

The colonel roared his disapproval. It was definitely a roar. Marian was not in the least distressed. She regarded her husband calmly and said, "I knew you would want to be certain that Miss Hawthorne was provided for, and for that it would be necessary to discover Mr. Hawthorne's circumstances, so I did. He left sufficient funds for her to have a few thousand pounds a year to live upon."

Outrage warred with curiosity; Mrs. Merriweather could see it on the colonel's face. She could also see that outrage was going to win and he was going to ring a peal over her head if she didn't forestall him quickly.

"Isn't it interesting, dear, that Mr. Hawthorne should have had so much saved? And yet lived so parsimoniously? Although, to be sure, Mr. Renfred did say Mr. Hawthorne did not know the extent to which his investments had prospered."

"Yes, but—"

"And don't you think it odd that he told his solicitor he meant to travel after his daughter was married, but he did his best to see that she never did?"

"Yes, but—"

"Please don't keep repeating yourself, dear, it's most unattractive."

"Marian, will you please stop that! You know very well you ought not to have gone jaunting off with Miss Hawthorne without telling me!"

Mrs. Merriweather fixed an innocent, wide-eyed gaze upon her husband's face. "Jaunt? I do not think I have ever jaunted in my life."

The colonel sputtered; he distinctly sputtered. "You know very well what I mean," he said when he finally collected himself sufficiently to be able to form the words. "You ought to have told me you were taking Miss Hawthorne to see her father's solicitor. Yes, and you ought to have taken me with you as well!"

"But my dear, I do not think she would have confided so openly in me if you had been there."

"That is not the point!"

Marian Merriweather reached up and stroked her husband's cheek. Her voice was soothing as she said, "Well, then, what is the point? That I might have been in some kind of danger by doing so? Nonsense! That it was improper? Mr. Renfred did not think so. Confess, my love. You are jealous that I stole a march on you and discovered something you could not."

"For heaven's sake, Marian! Two people are already dead! Do you wish to be the third? Or wish to risk that Miss Hawthorne might be?"

Mrs. Merriweather looked at her husband with an expression of fond exasperation upon her face. "Come now! Do you really believe that what we did was so dangerous? Surely, any place away from the museum would be as safe or safer than staying there? Except perhaps Hawthorne's house, and we didn't go there. But who is to know or care about Mr. Hawthorne's solicitor? The only person who stands to gain in any way from anything he could tell us is Miss Hawthorne, and surely you do not suspect her of killing her father or Tom? Indeed, you know that she could not have killed Tom because she was here, in this house, the night when it happened."

The colonel grumbled, but he had to grudgingly admit the truth of what she said. "I suppose you may be right when you say that it was a safe enough thing to do. Though if someone wished to remove you or Miss Hawthorne, they might try at any point that they found you alone."

"But why would anyone attack us?" Marian asked, ruthlessly pushing back the memory of looking into storage rooms at the museum.

"How the devil should I know?" the colonel demanded with some exasperation. "I don't even know why Hawthorne or Tom were killed in the first place! All I know is that you could be at risk. Suppose the person who killed Hawthorne thought his solicitor knew something and that by going there thought you had found out?"

Marian stared at him sardonically, and after a moment he sighed. "Very well. I suppose that even if it was somewhat risky, odds are that no one will ever know the two of you went there. Because you did say you were taking Miss Hawthorne shopping and you did have her purchase some new clothes. Very nice clothing, as I said before. You have excellent taste, my dear."

Mrs. Merriweather chuckled, relieved to have his attention diverted. "After twenty years of dressing obstinate young girls who hadn't the least notion of what would show them off to best advantage, I should think I would! To be sure, Miss Hawthorne is a trifle older than any of those girls were, but that simply made it an even more interesting challenge."

As she chattered on, Colonel Merriweather fixed his wife with a stern gaze. "Marian, are you attempting to distract me?" he demanded.

She smiled up at him. "Yes," she answered brightly.

"Thought so. But it won't work," he grumbled.

"No?" Marian smiled. Later she would tell him about the statue of the cat. But for now, she had other plans.

Again Marian touched the side of the colonel's face, then reached around to lightly pull his head down closer to her own. "Perhaps this would work better?"

And then, before he could object, even if he had been so foolish as to wish to do so, Mrs. Merriweather kissed the man she loved. Indeed, she distracted him so well for the next half hour that they were distinctly late going down to dinner! Lady Merriweather was not pleased.

# 11

Captain Stanfield halted in the doorway of the room that had become so familiar to him at the museum. For a moment he thought he must have taken a wrong turn, for though the pile of objects they had been sorting through was unmistakable, he did not recognize the fashionable young lady who sat with her back to the door.

"Pardon me," he said, coming forward. "Are you lost? May I be of assistance?"

It was only when she turned around and he noticed her spectacles that William realized he was looking at Ariel, that is to say, Miss Hawthorne. He must have said her name aloud, and with some astonishment in his voice, for she answered with some asperity.

"You needn't say it as though you find my appearance so incredible or ridiculous."

"N-not ridiculous in the least!" he managed to reply.

"Incredible then," she said, patently not mollified. "It was Mrs. Merriweather who insisted I visit a mantua maker, and I am well aware that I do not look like myself."

But by now Stanfield had recovered himself. He moved forward a trifle more quickly than usual and found himself a chair to draw up next to hers. He took her hand and held it tight when she would have snatched it away again. He looked into her eyes so that she could see the sincerity in his.

"I think you look wonderful," William said. "I was

taken by surprise, but it was surprise that I had not seen the lovely young woman hidden behind the bun fastened at the back of your neck, the ink-stained fingers, the spectacles, and the old-fashioned dresses you wore before."

"My fingers are as stained with ink as ever, my hair is still fastened in a bun at the back of my neck, and I am still wearing my spectacles," she replied in acid tones.

He smiled. "Yes, I know. And my fingers itch to remove your spectacles and undo the bun, perhaps even to gather your hair up into a topknot, so that the curls would fall about your face."

Miss Hawthorne pulled away in alarm, and this time she did manage to get her hand free. "You will do no such thing!" she exclaimed.

"No such thing as what?" a stern voice demanded from the doorway of the room.

Both William and Miss Hawthorne turned to see who was there. He recovered first. He managed a half-seated bow. "Mrs. Merriweather! I understand you are the hand behind Miss Hawthorne's transformation. I was informing her how delightful I found the change."

"And offered to change my hair as well," Miss Hawthorne added when he did not.

Mrs. Merriweather came forward, toward them. "Indeed? Most improper, sir, as well you should know! And if you recollect that I was once governess to your cousin, then you ought to have known better than to speak in such a way to any young lady who is in any way in my charge."

"Yes, Miss Tibbles, er, Mrs. Merriweather," William said with a meekness that deceived no one in the room.

But then, given the smile she could scarcely suppress, Mrs. Merriweather did not deceive anyone with her apparent sternness either.

The colonel was another matter. He entered the room a few short minutes after his wife, and he did not seem to be in the best of moods. He called them all laggards and insisted they should get to work at once!

"Yes, my dear," Mrs. Merriweather said with placid good humor. "I collect too many of the doors are locked and no one can find the keys?"

The color of the colonel's face betrayed the truth of this suggestion. "Seems the keys disappeared the day Mr. Hawthorne was killed. You do not know where they are, do you, Miss Hawthorne?" he asked.

Miss Hawthorne hesitated and exchanged looks with Mrs. Merriweather. "No," she said. "I have not seen Papa's keys since before he died. Not the set he wore on the chain of his watch fob, at any rate. I believe the spare set of keys is still at our old house."

"Well, would you be so good as to fetch them?" the colonel asked impatiently. "I meant to ask you for them yesterday, but I forgot."

"Of course. I shall go at once. I wish to be of any assistance I can," Miss Hawthorne replied.

"I should go with you," William said, rising to his feet as she did so.

"Yes, I do not like the notion of Miss Hawthorne going there alone," Mrs. Merriweather seconded the notion. "You may use our carriage to go and come back."

Miss Hawthorne hesitated, clearly not wishing to cause a fuss. But after a moment, she agreed. "I should be grateful for your escort," she told William. "It is foolish of me, I know, but I cannot be comfortable walking into that house alone. I keep thinking of Papa and half expecting him to be there with me. And after we found someone there, that first day . . ."

"I understand."

She slowed her steps to his, as he hobbled along beside her, leaning heavily on his cane. Nor did she show the slightest impatience at needing to do so. It was one more thing William found he liked so much about her. One more reason to be grateful for the time spent in her company.

Except that he didn't want to enjoy her company. He ought not to be personally involved with anyone here at the museum. Not when he had a job to do. Thornsby was already impatient with him that he had not yet accomplished what he had been sent here to do. Time was running short.

However foolish it might be, Stanfield couldn't help but care that Miss Hawthorne looked far more tired than he would like. There was a sadness about her that was only to be expected, and yet he found himself wishing he could ease her distress.

And so, once they were settled in the Merriweathers' carriage, William set out to charm Miss Hawthorne. He told her stories about the losses in his own life. He had felt dearly his own father's death, some few years before. And he told her how each death of a fellow soldier in the field had seemed to take a toll on him as well.

Under ordinary circumstances he would never have considered speaking of such intimate things with anyone, much less a young lady. But somehow Miss Hawthorne wasn't like other young ladies. She did not fall into hysterics nor hang upon his every word. Instead she spoke with sense and with sensibility. She entered into his sentiments even as he entered into hers, and as he talked, William felt some of his own pain ease. It was almost with a sense of wonder that he realized they had reached Mr. Hawthorne's house, for it seemed much too soon.

The couple Colonel Merriweather had hired greeted them at the door and then left them alone to find the keys. It did not take long. They were where Miss Hawthorne expected them to be, in her father's study.

She would have left at once to return to the museum, but William stopped her with a gesture. "May I," he asked hesitantly, "look through these books a bit? And perhaps glance at whatever it was your father was working on?"

"Why?" she replied, clearly taken aback by his odd demand.

William colored up, feeling unaccustomedly clumsy. "I, er, that is to say . . . In the short time that I knew your father, Miss Hawthorne, I came to respect him greatly. I should like to know better who he was, and I can think of no better way than through the books he chose for his library and the papers he wished to write."

She hesitated a moment, but then she nodded. "Of course. I understand. I have often felt the same. That his books and papers reflected precisely who he was, I mean. I shall leave you alone and go speak to Mr. and Mrs. Dearborn. They have been very kind to me and to have stayed in the house to take care of it while I have been gone, and I wish to thank them."

It was William's turn to say, "Of course."

He waited until she had left the room and then began to rapidly go through the drawers of her father's desk and the papers that lay on top of it. When he found nothing useful there, he began to pull books from the shelf at random and flip through them to see if anything fell out. To his great disappointment, nothing did so.

He heard her footsteps coming down the hallway, and by the time Miss Hawthorne came into the room, he was seated once again behind Hawthorne's desk, holding a pamphlet in his hand. She smiled at the sight of it.

"Pure sensationalism, Papa used to say. As if we could possibly know for certain how they lived in those days," Miss Hawthorne said tartly.

"And yet, your father spent his life trying to make his own guesses on that score, didn't he?" William countered.

She nodded, and a look of distress crossed her face. He felt an ogre for causing it. And yet he had to know, had to ask more questions of her.

"What did your father plan for the museum?" he asked. "What was his vision of how things could be?"

Now the smile Miss Hawthorne gave him was a far brighter one. "Papa said the trustees would soon arrange to build a new and larger home for the collections. It was his wish that more scholars could come and study what we have. Indeed, he meant to go to Egypt himself to collect more artifacts, for that was his particular favorite area of interest. For the moment, at any rate. His interests were apt to change with every new discovery.

Papa, I sometimes think, was interested in the entire world and everything in it."

William paused in the act of looking through a stack of papers on the desk. "Your father was going to go to Egypt?" he asked. "Had the museum agreed to send him?"

Miss Hawthorne looked away and bit her lower lip, as though sorry she had spoken so freely.

"Is something wrong?" William asked.

At first he thought she wouldn't answer him, but then she took a deep breath and said, "No. My father, it seems, had set aside some money and invested it so that there would have been enough for him to go."

William stared at her, and he knew his jaw hung open. He had seen how shabbily both Hawthorne and his daughter dressed. He had heard Hawthorne complain about minor expenses. Certainly he had never given any indication that he had sufficient funds saved for something like a journey to Egypt. So that was why Miss Hawthorne wore a new dress today. Clearly she had gotten access to the funds!

He must have spoken aloud, for Miss Hawthorne flushed. And then she surprised him. There was almost an air of defiance about her as she said, "Papa left enough to provide quite nicely for me. It was far more than I would have ever guessed he had saved. And I have no notion how he did so, even with the investments that were made for him. Certainly he never told me about any of it. But now the money is mine, and I need not live quite so penuriously as he chose to do."

William carefully eased himself up and moved to stand next to her. "When did you find out about the funds? Do you know where they came from?"

Miss Hawthorne smiled sadly and shook her head. "I have already said I do not. Indeed, I only know about the money at all because Mrs. Merriweather suggested I consult my father's solicitor yesterday to discover my circumstances. She was worried, you see, that I might need to earn my way, and thought it best I know as soon as possible. And when I saw Papa's solicitor, he told me about my inheritance. He said something about investments, but I do not know what sort they might have been."

William drew in a deep breath. "So you are a wealthy young lady, after all."

"You say that as though it makes a great difference," Miss Hawthorne said sharply. "Does it matter so much to your opinion of me, sir?"

He shook his head. "No. But I cannot help thinking it makes a very great difference to you, Miss Hawthorne. You will have your choice of suitors and of futures, in a way that you would not, if your father had left you destitute, as I half expected he might have done."

She unbent a trifle, then. "That is very much what Mrs. Merriweather has said to me," she admitted reluctantly. "But it is something I have not yet become accustomed to, and it feels very strange."

William nodded. "So it would, to anyone. Well, you will not need to work at the museum any longer. That must be something of a relief to you."

Miss Hawthorne rounded on him then. "Do you think I do so for money?" She paused and laughed bitterly. "I have not been paid so much as a halfpenny in all the years I helped Papa at the museum. I am considered a nuisance more than anything else by most of the people there. No, I go because I cannot bear not to do so! And your words only remind me that sooner or later, and I fear it shall be sooner, they will tell me that I am no longer welcome to be there."

And then she promptly burst into tears. William felt helpless. Her pain seemed to tug at his own heart. He knew it was not wise, but he could not simply step back and let her cry. Instead, he leaned his cane against the desk and put his good arm around Miss Hawthorne's shoulders. He drew her against his breast, as he had done once before. To himself he thought wryly that if he had wanted to court Miss Hawthorne, then he was not doing a very good job of appearing the heroic figure to her.

But he could not think what else to do except to simply hold her as she cried.

And, in the end, Miss Hawthorne rewarded him by lifting her head and gifting him with a tremulous smile. She even reached up and placed a gentle kiss against his cheek before moving away. William found himself oddly reluctant to let her go.

For a moment she kept her back to him, and then she turned and said in a brisk voice that fooled neither of them, "We had best get back to the museum with my father's keys. At least they were still here. The colonel and Mrs. Merriweather will be wondering what has happened to us."

"Yes, of course," he said, though he wished very much he could just stay there, with her, offering her as much comfort as she could or would accept.

But then, since that wasn't what he was supposed to be doing, perhaps it was just as well she insisted on going. Certainly William betrayed none of his feelings on his face or in his voice as he went outside with Miss Hawthorne.

In the carriage, going back to the museum, she worried how long they had been away and whether, perhaps, the colonel would be impatient with them. But perhaps they were not gone as long as it seemed, for neither the colonel nor Mrs. Merriweather made any comment to that point. Instead, they talked about the artifacts they had sorted through while Miss Hawthorne and Stanfield were gone.

William scarcely heard them. He was trying to decide how best he could carry out the job he'd been assigned by Thornsby without arousing the suspicions of the others. In the end he simply said quietly, "I am a trifle tired. If you will forgive me, I think I shall go home."

When they offered to accompany him out to the street, Stanfield held up a hand. "No, no, I shall be fine. Please go on with the work. As you have said, Miss Hawthorne, we don't know for how long they shall allow us to do so."

But the colonel would not be dissuaded. He walked

with the captain, and the moment they were out of ear-shot of the ladies, William discovered why Merriweather had been so persistent.

"Have you thought any more about what I said the other day?" the colonel asked.

"W-what do you mean?" William stammered.

"I mean, have you decided whether or not you wish to confide in me? You really should trust me, you know."

Stanfield stopped and drew himself upright. "I wish I could," he replied honestly. "I wish I could."

Colonel Merriweather stared at him and then gave a snort of disgust. He turned on his heel and stalked away, leaving William alone at the top of the stairs beside the stuffed giraffes that greeted visitors to the museum. Slowly Stanfield began to make his way down those stairs.

He half expected someone else to come and speak to him, but no one did. William went out the door, across the courtyard, and out the gate. Only when the porter would have hailed a hackney for him, did Stanfield pretend to remember something and go back inside, hoping that any watchers had by now turned away. He kept to the shadows, as much as he could, as he made his way back into the building. When he was certain no one was there to see him, he headed toward the part of the museum that so interested Thornsby.

# 12

The colonel returned to the room where Mrs. Merriweather and Ariel were working. They seemed to be deep in conversation, and he had to clear his throat quite loudly for them to notice his return.

"Perhaps it is just as well," he said, when he had their attention, "that Captain Stanfield has left. Mrs. Merriweather told me, last night, about the statue of the cat, Miss Hawthorne. I should like to see both it, and the room that contains it, for myself."

They made a small procession going through the museum, and Ariel could only be grateful that no one saw them, for she had no wish to answer questions to anyone save the colonel and Mrs. Merriweather. Not when she did not know who had taken the original statue.

When they reached the room, the colonel took out the spare set of keys Ariel had fetched from home. He unlocked the door, and much like Mrs. Merriweather had done, stood there for some moments just studying the room.

In a quiet voice, Mrs. Merriweather explained about the footprints they had found and how the room had been unlocked at the time although it shouldn't have been. Then, like Mrs. Merriweather, the colonel indicated that Ariel should precede him.

"There may be many such items in this room," she said quietly, "but this is the one I am most certain of."

As the older couple watched, Ariel lifted the box off

the shelf. As she opened it for the colonel she said, "It
is a clever imitation of the original, but that one had a
flaw right here and this one does not."

The colonel nodded his understanding as he carefully
took the statue and turned it over and around in his
hands. There was a grim look upon his face that only
deepened, the longer he looked at the thing.

As he did so, Mrs. Merriweather asked Ariel, "Have
you any notion, my dear, who would take the statue, or
why or where it might be sold? I know that you said
yesterday that you did not. But I thought perhaps something might have occurred to you overnight."

Ariel shook her head. "I only wish I had."

Mrs. Merriweather then turned to the colonel. "Well?"
she asked.

He nodded. "You are right, my dear," he said. "This
is important. And I know someone who will wish to
know about it at once."

Mrs. Merriweather did not try to hide her sense of
satisfaction. "I knew you would think it important," she
said. "So, what should we do next? Should we look for
more such imitations?"

That gave the colonel pause. He set down the object
and turned to her. His expression was stern as he said,
"You will do nothing of the sort! You are to go back to
my aunt's house, and I want you to take Miss Hawthorne
with you. I shall stay and investigate, but I want to know
that both of you are safe! This statue, or rather this false
statue, proves that something very dangerous is going
on here."

"I should have thought that two dead bodies did so
already quite effectively," Mrs. Merriweather countered
in a dry, angry voice.

"Yes, but this explains why. Now go back home. I
shall send word of this to someone who will come and
look at the statue and know precisely what to make of
it," the colonel said briskly.

Mrs. Merriweather started to object and then changed

her mind. Instead she looked at Miss Hawthorne and pondered the matter for a moment. Long enough for the colonel to become both suspicious and alarmed.

"Here, now, no more tricks, Marian! You are to go back to my aunt's house and you are to take Miss Hawthorne with you and you are not to do any more investigating on your own. Have I made myself clear?"

Mrs. Merriweather reached up and patted her husband's cheek. "Quite clear, my dear. Miss Hawthorne? Come along. We can do nothing more here, and I suppose we may as well go back to Lady Merriweather's house."

"Ma'am?" Ariel said, with a sense of understandable bewilderment.

"Marian!"

The colonel's voice held a warning. It was distinctly a warning and one that neither lady could mistake. Mrs. Merriweather looked at her husband, a bland expression upon her face. "Yes, my dear?"

"Straight back to my aunt's house!"

"Yes, dear."

He watched her, clearly distrustful, but he let them both go. Mrs. Merriweather was careful to say not a word until they were some distance from the room, and Ariel took her cue from the older woman. But when they were out of earshot she said, somewhat doubtfully, "Are we going straight back to Lady Merriweather's house?"

Before the other woman could answer, they spotted someone familiar at the far end of the corridor. He spotted them at the same moment and tried to slip back out of sight. But neither lady was having any such nonsense. They both began to run down the corridor and were in time to see the tip of a cane just before it disappeared inside a doorway.

Mrs. Merriweather and Miss Hawthorne looked at each other with grim smiles of satisfaction. Together they slowed their pace and moved silently toward that particular room. Aloud they began to talk.

"Isn't it a pity that the colonel wishes us to go home?"

"Yes, indeed. Do you know, I thought I saw Captain Stanfield, but perhaps I was mistaken?"

"Oh, yes, you must have been mistaken, Mrs. Merriweather, for we know he left some time ago."

"Yes, quite some . . ."

At that moment, they stepped into the room and stopped. It appeared to be empty, but neither Ariel nor Mrs. Merriweather was deceived. They could see marks in the dust on the floor. Mrs. Merriweather took up where she had left off.

". . . time ago. A pity, for we could have asked him about those things we were not certain where to place."

"Er, yes."

Ariel spied the tip of his boot just showing past the stack of boxes behind which he must be hiding. She signaled to Mrs. Merriweather and together they crept closer. Together they blocked any possible route of escape.

"Couldn't you, Captain Stanfield," Mrs. Merriweather said, stepping into his line of sight, "explain a number of things? Such as why you are hiding here, when you said you were leaving the museum some time ago."

She crossed her arms over her chest and waited. Captain Stanfield colored up a bright red, but he did not concede defeat easily. "I see you have found me out. I did mean to leave, but then thought that if I could just find a quiet place to rest for a bit I would be able to come and help again, and I would have saved myself the trip to my rooms and back."

"Oh, of course. Quite a sensible thing to do," Mrs. Merriweather said as though she believed him. "Don't you think so, Miss Hawthorne?"

Ariel stared at the captain. It shouldn't hurt this much to see him behave in such an odd way, but it did. She didn't want to believe him capable of anything infamous, but she could not help but wonder why he was lying to them, and felt hurt that he wished to lie to her. Mrs. Merriweather must know as well as she did that he was lying, and therefore there must be some meaning to what she said. Ariel gamely tried to follow the older woman's lead.

"I, yes, of course," the younger woman said, a bit doubtfully. "Most sensible."

"A pity," Mrs. Merriweather went on, "that I don't believe a word of it."

"Why the devil not?" Stanfield burst out.

"Because if it were that simple you would not have run away from us," Mrs. Merriweather said, advancing upon the hapless lad. "And you did run away and hide in here. Not very well, I must say, but the point is that you attempted to do so. It is not your fault that we were more observant than you counted upon. Now, Captain Stanfield, I should like the truth!"

He held his ground; Ariel had to give him that. Indeed, he straightened to his full height and even managed a wry smile. "I can see," he told Mrs. Merriweather, "why you were such an effective governess to my cousin. She didn't stand a chance, once you came upon the scene, did she?"

"No," the older woman agreed tranquilly, "and neither do you. So you may as well stop wasting our time and tell me the truth."

But before he could answer, Ariel stepped between Stanfield and Mrs. Merriweather.

"I am certain Captain Stanfield has a perfectly good explanation for his behavior," she said bravely.

"I am certain he does," the former governess agreed. "The only question is whether he means to tell us what it is. The truth, Captain Stanfield!" she repeated.

He sighed. "Very well, I thought to try to find out something on my own about your father's death, Miss Hawthorne. And about Tom's."

"Why not leave it to the Bow Street Runner, Mr. Collins?" Mrs. Merriweather asked suspiciously.

"Because he does not seem to be succeeding. Nor do I think Mr. Collins will ever put any effort into discovering who killed poor Tom. Your father's death he will perhaps investigate thoroughly, Miss Hawthorne, but not Tom's. And I happen to think his life mattered, too."

Suspicion warred in Ariel's breast with a desire to hug the captain for his concern about Tom. And since that was unthinkable, she stepped back and forced herself to say, "Well, and what have you found? And why hide from us?"

He looked at her then, and it seemed there was both honesty and pain in his eyes as he said, "I did not want you drawn into this, Miss Hawthorne. As for what I have found"—he paused, then seemed to force himself to go on—"I believe I have found evidence that someone is systematically looting artifacts from the museum. In some cases, I believe they may be replacing the originals with clever imitations in hopes that the thefts will go undetected that much longer."

Mrs. Merriweather began to tap her foot. "Have you any proof of this? And if so, just how did you discover it?" she demanded.

Captain Stanfield seemed to choose his words with care. He looked at Ariel. "Er, your father's keys did not precisely disappear. I took them in hopes of being able to return and investigate on my own, after hours. I looked in some of the storerooms and have seen some things that I cannot believe are genuine."

Ariel wanted to believe him. With the loss of both Tom and her father, she badly felt the need for something, someone to hold on to and believe in right now. Mrs. Merriweather was clearly more cynical, and in any event, made of far sterner stuff.

"You had the keys," the former governess said. "And you say that you wished to investigate after hours. Does that mean that you encountered Tom unexpectedly? That perhaps you were the one who killed him?"

"No!"

Captain Stanfield's shock and indignation seemed genuine. For the first time, Mrs. Merriweather's suspicions of him seemed to waver. "But you were here that night?"

"I meant to be," Stanfield admitted. "But another matter required my attention and I did not make it to the museum until morning. You saw me when I arrived. And though we did not discover his body until later, the Runner, Mr. Collins, is convinced that Tom was already dead." He paused and looked Mrs. Merriweather straight in the eyes. "That is one of the reasons why I feel such a responsibility to discover who killed Tom. If I had come when I intended, perhaps I could have prevented his death."

Mrs. Merriweather held out her hand. "Give me the keys," she said.

He shook his head and backed away.

"As proof of your good intentions," she persisted.

"No. I need them."

"Need them for what?" a voice asked from the doorway behind all of them. Then, "Marian, what the devil are you and Miss Hawthorne still doing here? I thought I told you both to go back to my aunt's house! What are you still doing here, bothering the poor boy this way?"

# 13

For a moment, all anyone could do was gape at the colonel. He came forward and stared hard at Captain Stanfield. "I suppose you work for Thornsby," he said, and it was not entirely a question.

"Andrew?" Mrs. Merriweather said with some uncertainty.

"Who is Thornsby?" Ariel asked, feeling as though her head were spinning, but determined to know the truth.

Stanfield flushed. He looked as if he wished to be anywhere but where he was. Since that was not possible, he took a deep breath, looked at the colonel, and nodded.

Colonel Merriweather sighed. "I hoped you would come and tell me yourself. I gave you the chance not half an hour ago. But you wouldn't trust me, would you?"

"If you know that I work for Thornsby, then you know that I could not," Captain Stanfield replied.

The two men stared at each other again, and this time it was the colonel's turn to nod his agreement. The two women were not pleased.

"Who is Thornsby?" Ariel repeated, beginning to grow more and more indignant at all these revelations.

"It's best you don't know," both the colonel and Captain Stanfield said at precisely the same moment.

"I suppose you will tell *me* the same thing?" Mrs. Merriweather demanded of both of them.

The two men nodded, and Ariel could see that the older woman was furious. Well, that made two of them.

It was time to let these two men know that they could not continue to prevaricate in such a way.

"If you do not tell me the truth," she said, "I shall go to the trustees and tell them that both of you are behaving in a most suspicious manner and ought to be banned from the museum premises," Ariel said, taking a step forward. "And don't think I am making an idle threat. I have done so before, and they did listen to me."

Was that approval she saw in Mrs. Merriweather's eyes? Ariel did not have time to ask. Instead, she continued to glare at the two men. "Well?" she demanded. "Do you mean to tell me the truth, or do I arrange to have you both barred from the museum?"

"If you do so, who will investigate your father's and Tom's deaths?" the colonel protested.

"Mrs. Merriweather and I shall do so," Ariel retorted, not allowing herself to be swayed. "I am certain that between us we can do everything necessary to catch whoever killed my father and Tom."

That threat worked as the other one had not. Both men began to speak with great haste, and the words seemed almost to tumble over each other.

"Here, now! That wouldn't be safe! You must leave it to us!"

"You've no notion what is going on! The risks you would be taking!"

"We know, er, that is, I think we both know things you and Mrs. Merriweather do not."

"Marian, be sensible! Tell Miss Hawthorne how foolish she is to say such nonsense!"

Everyone paused long enough to look at Mrs. Merriweather expectantly. She stared from one to the other, then said calmly, "We are waiting, Miss Hawthorne and I, for an explanation. And if we do not get one, I shall go with her to speak to the trustees. And help her to investigate. However much the two of you may wish to keep us out of this, you cannot do so. Neither Miss Hawthorne nor I will allow it."

The two men looked at each other, not troubling to

hide the annoyance they felt. For a moment Ariel thought they were going to blame each other for the situation in which they found themselves. Then they both sighed, and the colonel turned and went out the door. The two women waited. After checking the corridor, Merriweather returned and closed the door so that they could not be overheard.

And then the colonel began to explain. Ariel listened, but took what she heard with some skepticism. For she did not in the least doubt that both men would lie if they felt it would serve their purpose or if they thought they could do so without getting caught.

"We are both, Captain Stanfield and I, here because we were asked to look into a situation at the museum," Merriweather said. "Stanfield's, er, superior, Thornsby, and in my case, Hawthorne, both suspected that someone was stealing artifacts from the museum and wished us to see what we could discover. Is that not correct, Captain Stanfield?"

"Yes, quite correct, Colonel Merriweather, though how you knew about Thornsby—"

"Experience, my boy. Now, Marian, Miss Hawthorne, we believe that the same persons stealing artifacts are responsible for the deaths of Mr. Hawthorne and Tom. Once he sees the artifact, the expert I told you about may be able to give us a starting point for tracking down the thieves."

"Which artifact?" Captain Stanfield demanded, leaning forward.

Ariel looked at him as if he were a stranger. At the moment, it seemed very much as if he were. She forced aside the hurt and coolly described the statue of the cat, as well as where it was to be found.

Stanfield let out a sigh of frustration and ran his good hand through his hair. "I missed that one! I must send a message to, er, my superior," he said. "As soon as possible. He must be informed as to what's been discovered here. And to the fact that you are now all privy to what I am doing here," he added wryly.

The colonel's voice was as cool as Miss Hawthorne's had been. "Oh, I've no doubt he will want to know all about this. By all means send him a message."

"Never mind that," Mrs. Merriweather said impatiently. "So far, you have told us very little that we did not already know, or at the very least, guessed. What we should like to know is what happens next!"

"What happens next," both men said together, "is that you ladies go to Lady Merriweather's house and stay out of things! Leave the investigation to us!"

Ariel wanted to argue. She could see that Mrs. Merriweather did, too. But it was quite evident that they would not be allowed to do anything useful today anyway, so, with poor grace, she moved toward the door.

Over her shoulder she said, "Come, Mrs. Merriweather. Let us leave these men to their games."

As though they did not trust them, Captain Stanfield and the colonel escorted Ariel and Mrs. Merriweather out of the museum. There they handed both ladies into the Merriweathers' carriage and the colonel directed his coachman to drive them straight to Lady Merriweather's town house.

As the carriage pulled forward, Mrs. Merriweather patted Ariel's hand. "You may as well get used to how men think, my dear. They are forever trying to protect us when they ought to be asking our advice."

"I do not like it," Ariel retorted.

Mrs. Merriweather smiled, and it was not a pleasant smile. "I do not like it either, my dear. Nor will the colonel be entirely happy with the results of his decree. But for now, we may as well accept what we cannot change."

That was all very well, Ariel thought, but it still did not make her happy. She consoled herself by telling herself that at least nothing further was likely to go wrong today. She found, however, when they got to the town house, that she had been mistaken.

Lady Merriweather was waiting and in alt. She seemed scarcely to notice that in one hand she held a novel and on her nose was perched a pair of spectacles even less flattering than Ariel's. All her attention was focused on the note in her hand.

"My dear," she said to Ariel, "you cannot know the treat in store for you!"

Ariel stared at her hostess, as much astonished at the sight of the spectacles as by Lady Merriweather's words. Alerted by the younger woman's stare, Lady Merriweather snatched the spectacles from her nose and peered nearsightedly at Ariel and Mrs. Merriweather. She also hid her novel, the latest rage in London, behind her back.

"Sly puss, why didn't you tell me you were on such terms with Lady Jersey?" Lady Merriweather demanded.

"What terms?" Ariel asked, completely bewildered.

"Such terms that Sally Jersey has chosen to hold a small gathering in your honor tonight! The invitation just arrived this hour past, and I accepted for all of us."

"But I am in mourning," Ariel protested.

"You will not be in mourning forever," Lady Merriweather snapped in reply. "And of all people, Sally Jersey is most likely to remember any real or imagined insult. This is to be a quiet evening; no dancing, no music or other entertainments, nothing more than a quiet evening among friends. Lady Jersey wrote that she has chosen to invite only people who knew your father, Miss Hawthorne. She says that she understands you have not been able to stay at your own home and receive callers who wish to express their sympathies to you, and so she thought she would provide an opportunity for them to do so, at her house, tonight."

"How kind of her," Mrs. Merriweather murmured. "I wonder how she knew Miss Hawthorne was here?"

"I don't know how she knew Miss Hawthorne was here," Lady Merriweather said with some exasperation. "But it does not signify! What does matter is that Lady Jersey has gone to a great deal of trouble, in a very short time, and it would be foolish to snub her for doing so.

And if Lady Jersey thinks it proper for Miss Hawthorne to attend, then it cannot possibly *be* improper.''

More bewildered than ever, Ariel looked to Mrs. Merriweather for support and advice. ''What shall I do?''

Mrs. Merriweather hesitated, as well she might, Ariel thought. But in the end she nodded slowly. ''Perhaps it might be considered not a party but rather just a wish to provide you with some comfort, and in that event, it would indeed be churlish to refuse. If we are mistaken, it will be a simple matter to leave at once. But I confess I am curious to know what is behind Lady Jersey's kindness.''

''Kindness?'' Ariel recoiled from the word. ''You call it kindness that she expects me to come and talk with people, some of whom I may not know, when all my thoughts are upon my father's and Tom's death? When I wish nothing more than to either curl up in my room alone, or to investigate and find out who did such a horrible thing!''

''Yes, kindness, and you should be grateful for Lady Jersey's condescension!'' Lady Merriweather said sharply.

Ariel looked from one to the other. Lady Merriweather displayed only impatience. Mrs. Merriweather, however, had a thoughtful look upon her face, and Ariel began to waver. Mrs. Merriweather seemed at once to sense the change in her. She reached out, took Ariel's arm, and gripped it with unmistakable urgency.

''Come, my dear. Let us go upstairs and choose which gown you will wear,'' the former governess said soothingly. ''Not that the mantua maker had that many to send home with us yesterday, but you will wish to look your best, and you will wish to wear something that clearly signals your state of mind. Be sensible, my dear,'' she added when Ariel would have protested further. ''You did say that your father did not wish you to go into mourning. If the people Lady Jersey has invited know that, they will be astonished at your impertinence in disregarding his wishes by not showing up!''

"But Mrs. Merriweather—" Ariel began.

Mrs. Merriweather gave her no chance to say more but started up the stairs, speaking straight over Ariel's voice. "Your deepest blue, I think. Or perhaps the very dark green silk will do. No jewelry, unless there are some ear bobs your father gave you that you have an attachment for? No? Then, as I said, no jewelry. Dark gloves, I think. How fortunate that we went shopping yesterday! Come along, dear. We haven't a moment to waste."

Ariel looked at Lady Merriweather, who looked ready to ring a peal over her head, then at the former governess, and decided to follow her upstairs. She sighed. There was a time to do battle, but right now she was too tired to fight this one. Besides, she found herself quite curious to know just why Mrs. Merriweather was so in favor of going.

And after all, if she misliked the looks of things when they got to Lady Jersey's house, Ariel told herself, she would simply find a quiet corner and stay there for the entire evening. And no one was going to change her mind about that!

Upstairs, however, she ventured to ask Mrs. Merriweather, "Why do you seem so eager to go tonight?"

The former governess smiled, but it was a very grim smile. "I think it odd," she said, "that Lady Jersey should go to such trouble for you, and upon such short notice. I cannot help but wonder if someone asked her to do so. If so, I think we may be certain the person will be there tonight and perhaps we may discover why. We may also discover whether your father confided his concerns about the museum to anyone else. And we may see whether anyone shows an unnatural interest in what *you* may know of your father's thoughts."

Ariel nodded. "Yes," she said slowly. "I see. But why would anyone think that I know anything?"

"We asked questions today at the museum. Perhaps someone even saw us yesterday in the storage room with the statue of the cat. Or perhaps it has to do with whatever reason caused someone to be at your house the day

your father died. Someone, that day, was after something, and that someone may believe that *you* know
where it is."

Again Ariel nodded. She watched as Mrs. Merriweather went through the new dresses and chose one for
Ariel to wear. "Here, this will suit you admirably. Dark
enough to not offend the sensibilities of those who do
believe in mourning, but not so grim as to offend those
who know your father forbade you to go into blacks.
And flattering enough to draw Captain Stanfield's eyes,
should he be there, as well."

"C-captain Stanfield?" Ariel stammered.

Mrs. Merriweather paused and looked at the younger
woman. "Yes, Captain Stanfield. You cannot pretend
you are indifferent to the fellow, for I have seen how
you look at him. And how he looks at you."

"Yes, but, we found him today hiding in that room.
The colonel said he had been keeping secrets from us,"
Ariel said doubtfully.

"And so he has," Mrs. Merriweather agreed. "But if
you think over what was said, the colonel appears to
know the man for whom Captain Stanfield is working.
And he said that the captain has been trying to discover
if there have been thefts at the museum. That is honorable, is it not?"

"Y-yes."

"And he regrets Tom's death and wishes he could help
discover who killed your father as well as Tom. That is
also honorable."

"Yes," Ariel agreed reluctantly. "But why did he not
confide in us? Why did he not confide in me?"

Mrs. Merriweather began to laugh, much to Ariel's
indignation. After a moment, she drew a breath, however, and said, "You must understand, my dear, that men
often feel they must keep secrets. Particularly from us. I
have no doubt that the captain felt he was protecting
you by not informing you why he was there. And I have
no doubt he felt it a matter of honor as well, since he
did not confide in the colonel, either, even when my

husband gave him the chance to do so again today. No, no, you must not let such a thing as that stop you from caring about the captain."

Ariel hesitated. She had so many questions that she scarcely knew where to begin. "Am I foolish," she said at last, "to allow myself to feel a *tendre* for the captain? Perhaps he is merely kind to me and feels nothing of the sort himself."

Mrs. Merriweather put a comforting arm around the younger woman's shoulders. "Oh, my dear! One cannot choose where the heart will care! One can only choose what one will do about it. I cannot tell you for certain how the captain feels. He has not confided in me, and in any event, if he is like most men, he does not even know himself how he feels. I can only tell you that he looks at you as if he cares. And he seems, moreover, to be a good and honorable man. Though I will grant you that he seems a trifle wanting in wits if he did not realize he could trust us and Colonel Merriweather!"

That made Ariel laugh. But then she paused. "Is that enough?" she asked. "Even if he should return my regard, how would I know whether what I felt was love? How will I know, whether it be Captain Stanfield or someone else, if this is a man with whom I should choose to spend my life?"

It was Mrs. Merriweather's turn to hesitate. "If you had to marry, if your father had left no provision for you, I might answer you differently. But as matters stand, you certainly need not settle for just any man who asks for your hand in marriage."

Mrs. Merriweather paused and stepped away from Ariel to pace about the room. After a moment, she turned, faced her, and took a deep breath. "I cannot tell you, my dear," she said, "how to be certain that what you feel is love. What I do think matters as much, or perhaps even more, is how you feel about yourself when you are with a man—whether it be Captain Stanfield or anyone else. Do you feel you must become someone else to please him, or are you able to be who you truly are? Do you like the qualities he encourages in you?"

"The colonel objects when you try to investigate," Ariel pointed out doubtfully.

"Yes, but he knows he cannot truly stop me," Mrs. Merriweather replied. "He simply worries, as I worry about him. Nor do I let his concerns stop me from doing what I feel I must. If I did, then *that* would be something to worry about!"

"Why must it be so complicated?" Ariel asked in evident frustration.

"I suppose," Mrs. Merriweather said consolingly, "because we are complicated creatures, men and women alike. Just be grateful that you do have a choice, my dear. Be grateful that your circumstances do not force you to choose between taking a position such as governess or marrying someone you do not love. Now, come. We must finish choosing what you will wear tonight. A bit of Lady Merriweather's vanity might not be misplaced, on such an occasion as this. Must you, do you think, wear those spectacles?"

"Yes," Ariel said firmly, "I must."

# 14

Ariel wore the spectacles. "My father's friends wouldn't recognize me if I didn't," she said, as if that settled the matter.

Lady Jersey greeted them warmly. To Ariel she said, "I used to have a *tendre* for your father, you know. He was such a handsome fellow in his youth! I daresay half the girls I knew had a *tendre* for him. But once he saw your mother, there was no catching his eye for any of the rest of us. It is such a pity your father turned his back upon society after your mother died. He was always haring off to strange places, wasn't he? At any rate, when I heard that he was dead and you were left alone, I knew I had to do something to make his poor daughter feel welcome among the *ton*. My dear, why on earth did he never bring you out?"

Ariel didn't know quite what to say. "I, that is to say, Papa thought it unimportant. He needed my help at the museum, you see."

That prompted a cry of outrage from Lady Jersey. "Well, in my opinion," she said sternly, "your father used you shamelessly! What was he thinking? How did he ever expect you to find a husband there? Although I have heard rumors that you managed to catch the eye of at least one eligible gentleman! But I am putting you to the blush and I never meant to do so, I promise you! So never mind. Come and meet the rest of my guests. I make no doubt some of them are known to you already, but in addition to your father's friends and colleagues, I also invited a few ladies who may be able to smooth your way in society, if they so choose. Don't worry. I shall introduce to you everyone who is not already known to you. A pity about the spectacles. I suppose you must wear them? Comes of reading too much, I daresay. Your father wouldn't have thought of that, either. A handsome man, but one without a dash of common sense about him."

Her head slightly in a whirl, Ariel allowed herself to be led about the room by Lady Jersey. The colonel and Mrs. Merriweather came as well, though Lady Merriweather moved off to greet one of her bosom bows.

"How did you come to think of this kindness to Miss Hawthorne?" Mrs. Merriweather asked.

Lady Jersey blinked at her. "Do you know, I cannot recall. I simply remember hearing about Mr. Hawthorne's death and knowing I must do something for his daughter. Ah, here we are. Miss Hawthorne, I believe you have not yet met Lady Hadwin? Lady Hadwin, may I make Miss Hawthorne known to you?"

And so it began. It was, as promised, a quiet evening. There was no music or other entertainment, just a chance to talk. Everyone seemed bent upon being kind to Miss Hawthorne, either because of their affection for her father or from fear of incurring Lady Jersey's disapproval if they were not.

In spite of herself, Ariel found she was glad she had come. She had not known her father had so many friends among the *ton*. Nor had she known how highly even those who were not scholars seemed to think of him. Why, then, had he never taken her with him when he was invited to one place or another? It was a question no one seemed able to answer.

Somewhat to her surprise, Ariel discovered that Captain Stanfield had been invited, along with his mother. Oddly enough, the woman seemed most interested in meeting her. Stanfield seemed equally bent upon helping Ariel avoid her. To that end, he betrayed himself by staying almost a constant companion at Ariel's side and guiding her about the room so that for most of the evening his mother had no chance to speak to her.

It was not that Ariel disliked Captain Stanfield's company. Indeed, she found it more than a little comforting to have him by her side. But it could only result in precisely the sort of gossip he seemed most eager to avoid. If his mother had been interested in her before tonight, she would be far more so after it.

But Ariel could not bring herself to send Captain Stanfield away. He seemed to know just what to say when the words of these strangers threatened to overset her composure. He seemed to know just how and when to ward them off from even approaching her.

"Are you all right?" he asked after they had been there for some time.

Ariel nodded. "Yes, and I thank you for your help. It is not easy for me to be here."

Captain Stanfield looked around. "I cannot understand what Lady Jersey was thinking," he said impatiently. "But where she commands, few are willing to refuse to go. So we all are here. But I promise you that I shall do my best to shield you from anyone you wish."

Ariel smiled up at him wistfully. She wished he could guard her from the weaknesses of her own heart. It was not her grief over her father that she wished he could take away, for that was welcome, if only because it still kept her feeling connected to Papa.

No, it was this unwelcome tug she felt every time she looked up into Stanfield's face, every time she felt his comforting hand on her shoulder. Who was going to protect her from this unaccustomed need that seemed to grow stronger each time she saw him, each time he did something that showed his attention to her comfort in a way that no one, not even Mama or Papa, had ever shown before?

Mrs. Merriweather seemed to think it was a good

thing, this feeling, but Ariel was not so certain. It was
far too unsettling. There were moments when she felt as
though these feelings might overwhelm her. And she did
not, when Captain Stanfield smiled at her in such a reassuring way, trust her own common sense. And that was
more disconcerting than anything else!

Still, it was comforting to have him beside her as she
talked with those who had known her father. Ariel even
learned to accept with something that at least gave the
appearance of equanimity, the compliments on her person. She was not accustomed to hearing herself described
as a lovely young lady. Intelligent, yes, but except from
Papa it had never been meant as a compliment. And any
comments about her appearance had more likely been
an instruction to change an ink-stained skirt than to ap-
plaud her efforts to appear to advantage.

"William, go fetch Miss Hawthorne a glass of ratafia,"
a woman commanded.

Ariel looked up and realized that this was Stanfield's
mother. He did not seem pleased to see her standing
there. Nor pleased to see her then sit down on the sofa
beside Ariel, as if she meant to stay awhile. He hesitated,
but in the end he did as he was told, while his mother
settled her skirts about her and studied Ariel with
open curiosity.

"So you are the young lady who has dazzled my son,"
Lady Chadbourne said. "I wonder why."

"So do I," Ariel blurted out without thinking.

A peal of laughter escaped Lady Chadbourne, and she
grinned at Ariel. "I think I shall like you, my dear, which
is fortunate—under the circumstances."

"Circumstances?" Ariel asked warily.

"Oh, yes, the circumstances. Given my son's pointed
attendance upon you this evening, I think we may expect
some sort of pronouncement from him before much
longer. Indeed, perhaps"—she paused as a thought
struck her—"the two of you already have an understanding and he has just not seen fit to inform me of that
fact?"

Fascinated, Ariel shook her head. "No. We have no understanding. I do not know what his interest in me might be, other than his wish to carry on the work he was doing for my father and his knowledge that I can be of assistance to him in that."

Another peal of laughter escaped Lady Chadbourne, drawing even more interested looks than before. "Oh, my dear, you are a refreshing creature! Perhaps that is why my son is so fascinated with you! No, I promise you, it is not simply your father's work that interests my son. If it were only that, he would be very careful not to be seen so often in your company that talk must surely arise. He has, after all, been raised with a perfect understanding of the consequences of his behavior and what is proper under what circumstances."

"As I have not?" Ariel asked, a hint of defiance in her voice.

Lady Chadbourne patted her hand soothingly. "You have been raised by a scholar. And scholars are impractical creatures, as we all know. They have not the least understanding, or care, for what the *ton* might say. I daresay that however a good man your father was, he did not spare a great deal of thought for what might be best for you. Or perhaps he did not wish you to be approved by the *ton*. After all, if you were, he might lose a valuable assistant. And yes, I have heard how he had you work with him at the museum when he ought to have been seeing to your future instead."

"I will not hear a word said against Papa," Ariel said stiffly. "He was very dear to me."

"Well, of course he was!" Lady Chadbourne exclaimed, as though astonished that Ariel might think she believed otherwise. "I should be very disappointed in you if you did not feel such proper affection for your father. But that does not mean you must be blind to his faults. Nor that I should not sympathize at the ways they affected you."

Ariel had no notion how to answer that sally. And indeed, she greeted the reappearance of Captain Stanfield, and the glass of champagne in his hand, with far greater warmth than she might otherwise have done.

"I thought you might prefer this to ratafia," he told Ariel. Then he looked from her to his mother and said in a warning tone, "Mama?"

Lady Chadbourne rose to her feet slowly. She looked down at Ariel and smiled. "Come see me tomorrow, my dear. I should like to have the chance to speak with you in private. Have my son bring you."

And before either Stanfield or Ariel could protest her high-handed orders, she moved away and they were left staring at each other, the beginnings of a smile turning up the corners of their mouths.

"My mama is, er, a very forceful woman," Stanfield said apologetically.

"So I have seen," Ariel agreed. "What shall I do?"

"Go see my mother tomorrow. And I shall take you."

"You don't mind?" Ariel asked doubtfully.

He laughed, but it was a forced sound. "It would not matter if I did. But as it happens, no I do not mind. Let my mother weave her fantasies. I am the one member of the family she cannot command. It does no harm, therefore, to indulge her in these little matters upon occasion."

And then he did move away, leaving Ariel feeling bereft, and it was more than the simple absence of his person to act as guard against everyone who wished to speak with her. She could not help wondering whether he considered tomorrow's visit a little matter because he meant to propose, or because he thought her of so little consequence that it did not matter what expectations might be raised by his attentions to her.

There was no time, however, to worry over the question, because an older gentleman took the chair opposite her. He reached out and patted Ariel's hand awkwardly. She tried to smile.

"I am so sorry, my dear, to hear of your father's death," the gentleman said. "I am Mr. Kinkaid. Your father no doubt spoke of me—we were great friends."

He looked at her expectantly, and Ariel scarcely knew what to say. Her father had never mentioned this man, but then he had never mentioned most of the people who had spoken to her tonight. She knew of him, of course. Anyone involved in antiquities had heard his name as that of a collector, and not always a scrupulous one. In the end she merely smiled weakly at Mr. Kinkaid and let him draw his own conclusions.

"What is to become of your father's papers and researches? I ask, you see, because we were in some sort colleagues and—"

"And I should be be happy to look over whatever papers Miss Hawthorne's father may have left behind," another voice said smoothly.

Ariel looked up to see Lord Hollis, one of her father's friends, and felt an immense sense of relief. She was almost tempted to agree to his suggestion, but there was a gleam, an almost predatory gleam it seemed to her, in Lord Hollis's eyes that stopped her. Did everyone want to take over her father's work?

In the end Ariel said, "I believe Colonel Merriweather is going to perform that office for me. You might speak to him, if there was something in particular either of you wished to have or know about."

Lord Hollis didn't answer, but Kinkaid's gloved hands clenched the arms of the chair tightly, and it seemed there was anger now in his eyes. "Is that wise?" he asked, careful to keep his voice level. "There are certain, er, rumors about the colonel that might make one hesitate to entrust such an important task to his care."

Ariel drew in her breath. She also kept her voice level as she replied, "Perhaps, Mr. Kinkaid. But my father trusted him, and it was his wish that the colonel do so. Surely you would not wish me to contradict my father's dying wishes?"

Lord Hollis blinked. "Your father spoke before he died? That is to say, I had heard he was found dead."

"He was," a voice at Ariel's shoulder said calmly, and

a hand squeezed her shoulder in a way that gave her a surprising degree of comfort.

She looked up to see Colonel Merriweather standing behind her. He smiled down at her reassuringly. To Lord Hollis and Mr. Kinkaid he said, "Mr. Hawthorne was found quite dead, but he had talked earlier of how, should anything happen to him, he wished me to take care of his papers and such. It was almost as though he sensed something might happen to him."

"Indeed? Then of course you must do as he asked," Kinkaid said indifferently.

"I must say that it is very odd he did not ask for my assistance," Lord Hollis added stiffly, as though insulted, "but if he did not, he did not."

Kinkaid rose to his feet and bowed to Ariel. "Again, my dear, my sympathies on your father's death. It was a delight to meet you at last. Your father was very proud of you."

"Yes," Hollis agreed, "he was."

As both men walked away, Ariel found her eyes filling with tears. Was Papa proud of her? She wished that if he had been, he had been able to say so to her instead of just to his friends. It was the sort of thing she would have liked to know while he was alive.

As though he sensed her distress, the colonel squeezed her shoulder again. In a low voice that carried only to her ears he said, "Would you like to go, my dear? You look all done up, and we have certainly been here long enough to satisfy Lady Jersey. And if we have not, well I don't give a fig for what she may think!"

Ariel smiled at that sally. "Your aunt is not likely to agree. Still, I am tired and I should like to go, if we could," she admitted.

"Stay here and leave Lady Merriweather to me," the colonel replied. "I'll fetch both my wife and my aunt and deal with any objections they may have. We'll be home in a trice."

Ariel did not notice that Mr. Kinkaid had apparently

gone straight from talking with her to Mrs. Merriweather's side. Nor did she know that he wasted no time in coming to the point. "Mrs. Merriweather, forgive my presumption. I know that we have not been properly introduced. I am Mr. Kinkaid, and I have some interest in Mr. Hawthorne's work. I understand you have some interest and influence with Miss Hawthorne. May I strongly suggest that you advise Miss Hawthorne to take a trip away from London? Perhaps a nice, quiet visit to the countryside—somewhere far away from anything to do with her father's work? It would, in my opinion, be advantageous for her health."

"But—"

She got no further. Kinkaid bowed and was gone, just in time to avoid encountering Colonel Merriweather. It was a circumstance that did not escape the former governess's attention.

"What the devil was Kinkaid saying to you?" Colonel Merriweather demanded with a frown.

She told him. "Mr. Kinkaid bears watching," she concluded thoughtfully.

"Yes, but not tonight," the colonel replied firmly. "It is time to take Miss Hawthorne home. Let us collect my aunt and go."

If it was a little longer than the trice the colonel had promised, before they were home, it was not a great deal longer. The moment they returned to Lady Merriweather's town house, Ariel did not hesitate to seek her room. There, after being undressed and prepared for bed, she waited until the maid was gone and then she went to sit on the window bench, staring out at the night sky.

Her thoughts took two directions, both of which felt as though they might easily overwhelm her fragile state. The grief for her father betrayed itself in the tears that streamed down her face. It was nice, tonight, to see how many people had admired Papa, but it was also a reminder that there had been a side of him she had never seen and now never would have the chance to know.

The other direction her thoughts took was of Captain

Stanfield. What if he was beginning to feel for Ariel what she already felt for him? Was it so foolish to hope for that? To let herself believe that such a thing might be possible?

Eventually Ariel sought her bed, but it was hours before sleep managed to capture her, and dawn came and went unseen.

# 15

The colonel and Mrs. Merriweather regarded each other over the breakfast table. "Perhaps," he said slowly, "we have been too quick to refuse invitations while we are here in London, my dear."

"My thoughts precisely," she agreed. "Indeed, I have been thinking that I have shockingly neglected a number of friends and former charges. Why, look at all the interesting people we met last night."

"Yes, very interesting people," the colonel agreed. "And you know that your former girls would all like to see you, if any of them should chance to be in London right now. Perhaps you ought to pay some courtesy calls today."

"I was thinking the very same thing."

It was a perfectly ordinary conversation, the sort any couple might have over breakfast. But Ariel sensed far more going on than was being said aloud. She could not, however, ask when there were so many servants hovering with such great interest. Still, she was not in the least surprised when Mrs. Merriweather said to her, "Why don't you come with me today, Miss Hawthorne? I shall take you to call upon one or two ladies who might be of help to you in the future."

"But I am supposed to go see Lady Chadbourne today. Captain Stanfield is to come and take me there."

Mrs. Merriweather waved a hand. "That is this afternoon. We shall be back well in time for you to change your dress, if you wish, and make yourself ready to go."

Ariel tried again. "I am in mourning," she said quite reasonably. "I have no taste for visiting strangers, particularly when their drawing rooms are likely to be full of other visitors."

Mrs. Merriweather smiled kindly. "To be sure, I would enter into your sentiments completely, *if* I were planning to make ordinary calls. But I mean to send around messages asking if we may call early, before any other visitors might be expected to present themselves. And I assure you, these ladies will quite understand and sympathize with the wisdom in my introducing you to ladies in the *ton*. They are also quite likely to take you under their wings, so that when the colonel and I do leave London, you will not find yourself entirely without friends here. Oh, I know from last night that your father had a great many friends. And perhaps some of them would take you under their wings. I certainly hope they will do so. But that is not quite the same as having ladies almost your own age as friends. Ladies young enough to be able to enter into the sentiments you might feel."

Ariel wanted to protest, but it would have been churlish to do so. Mrs. Merriweather was trying to be helpful. She knew, moreover, even upon such short acquaintance with the former governess, that sooner or later Mrs. Merriweather would have her way. Was there anyone, she wondered, who had ever managed to stand up to the woman? Anyone who had ever refused to obey her commands?

She must have spoken aloud, for the colonel laughed. "Not that I have seen," he told her, a distinct twinkle in his eyes. "Mrs. Merriweather is quite a formidable woman."

Mortified, Ariel looked at the former governess, who, far from appearing offended, had a somewhat distant look in her eyes.

After a moment Mrs. Merriweather said, in a musing

voice, "There have been one or two fools who would not listen to me. As I recall, I had to bash one of them over the head, and another suffered even deeper regrets than that. Not that I would ever do, or need to do, such a thing to you, my dear! For one thing, you are not a villain, and for another, you have thus far shown the greatest good sense. Now, will you come along with me this morning?"

In spite of herself, Ariel laughed. It was impossible to withstand Mrs. Merriweather's determination or her charm. "Yes, I will come," she said. "But mind, we really must be back in time for me to go see Lady Chadbourne. It would not do to offend Captain Stanfield's mother."

"No, indeed," Colonel Merriweather said in a grave voice that was belied by the smile upon his face. "Marian, I strictly charge you to have her back here in time."

Mrs. Merriweather cast a withering look at her husband. "That, my dear, is not something I am likely to forget. Of course I shall have her back here in time. And now I had best go write those notes to send round. If I know these ladies, and I do, we shall have an answer straightaway and be able to call upon them within the hour."

With a sense of unreality, Ariel watched Mrs. Merriweather leave the room. The colonel smiled sympathetically, as if he knew just how she felt.

"Have some breakfast, my dear," he said in soothing tones. "You appear to have a very busy morning ahead of you, and you will be grateful for the sustenance."

Once again, Ariel did as she was told. Not because she was a spineless creature, but because his words made sense. She had seen enough of Mrs. Merriweather to know that once she had the bit between her teeth there would be no stopping her until she had accomplished her goals. And Ariel had to admit that, as odd as it seemed to her to pay calls when she was in mourning, Mrs. Merriweather had been a governess, and a very strict one to all accounts, so she was more likely to know what was proper than Ariel. More than that, there was a kindness in having some distraction from her grief over her father's and Tom's deaths and her nervous anticipation of this afternoon's encounter with Stanfield's mother.

So Ariel did as she was told and ate a far more substantial breakfast than she might otherwise have done. And by early afternoon, she was indeed very grateful she had done so.

It happened as they were leaving Lady Farrington's house. Mrs. Merriweather had just informed Ariel that they might finally return home. Colonel Merriweather's carriage was drawn up at the side of the street, waiting for them, but as the two ladies walked toward it, someone crashed into Ariel and Mrs. Merriweather. It was enough to knock both ladies into the street and straight into the path of a carriage whose driver seemed oblivious to the danger. He was springing his horses recklessly and there seemed no way to avoid being trampled.

Ariel heard shouts of horror and cries of dismay. She felt rather than saw Mrs. Merriweather falling toward the street beside her. There was no time to think, only to react. She reached out and grabbed for the diminutive governess and rolled with her, praying there was only one carriage racing down the street. She could not roll backward, for there was no time to do so, but she could roll forward. Ariel kept rolling forward until they reached the other side of the street. Fortunately, Mrs. Merriweather did not fight it but was content to roll with her.

Hands reached down to help them to their feet. Other hands steadied them, and more than one person asked if they were all right. Voices rose all around them. One was Colonel Merriweather's coachman, apologizing profusely for not having been able to protect them. Mrs. Merriweather assured the poor fellow that it had not been his fault.

Ariel blinked, trying to find her bearings. She reached for her spectacles, only to discover they were missing. When she looked about, she saw the shattered pieces of glass and twisted frame still in the road. She looked at

Mrs. Merriweather. The other woman, having reassured
the coachman, stared back, a grim look in her eyes.

"Are you all right?" the former governess asked.

Ariel nodded. "Yes, though my spectacles are hope-
lessly smashed to pieces."

"How fortunate, then, that you really don't need them
to see," Mrs. Merriweather replied briskly. Ariel gaped
at her, and the older woman went on. "I presume you
wore them because it caused your father's colleagues to
take you more seriously. And perhaps also because it
put a distance between you and any young man who
might otherwise show too great an interest in you. Am
I correct?"

"Yes," Ariel admitted after a moment's hesitation. "I
suppose I ought to have known you would guess. I only
hope that no one else has done so! But never mind that.
Are you all right?"

Mrs. Merriweather grimaced and put a hand to her
back. "Yes, though I fear I shall feel the effects of this
as the day goes on. I am too old for such nonsense."

As she spoke, Lady Farrington reached their side of
the street. Her face was very pale. "Miss Tibbles, are you
all right? What happened? From the window it looked as
if the both of you were pushed into the street!"

Mrs. Merriweather looked at her. "I wonder if we
might prevail upon your hospitality once again, Barbara,
to rest for a bit? And then," she added softly, "we may
discuss what happened in private."

Lady Farrington flushed. "Yes, of course, Miss Tibbles.
That is to say, Mrs. Merriweather. Please come back to
the house with me. And please be careful!"

All of them were extremely careful, alert for carriages
on the street, alert for anyone who might try the trick
again of pushing them. Colonel Merriweather's coachman was the most vigilant of all. It was clear from the
grim set of his jaw that he was determined not to allow
any further injury to come to the ladies.

Inside the house, Lady Farrington sent for brandy and

a basin of water so that Ariel and Mrs. Merriweather could make themselves presentable again.

"Are you really all right?" Lady Farrington demanded.

Mrs. Merriweather sighed. "No, and I doubt I shall be anytime soon. I, and Miss Hawthorne, will no doubt find ourselves covered with bruises by morning. I ache already. But beyond that, yes, we are all right. I should very much like to know, however, who pushed us, and precisely why."

"So should I," Ariel said grimly.

"Tell us everything you remember seeing from the window, Barbara," Mrs. Merriweather told her former student.

Lady Farrington did so. "I thought I saw a man—he seemed to be wearing a hat of some sort well pulled down on his head, so I cannot tell you what his features were like or even the color of his hair. He moved a little strangely, almost as if he was hunched over, and that was what first drew my attention to him. Then he seemed to move a little faster and shove against the pair of you. When I saw you fall toward the street, I left the window and ran down to see how you were so I saw nothing more."

Mrs. Merriweather grimaced. "I cannot blame you for that," she said. "In your place, I would have done the same. A pity, though, that you did not see enough to let us determine who the man might have been, or at least to try to find him again."

"Could it not have been an accident?" Lady Farrington asked cautiously. "I know that I said it looked as if you had been pushed, but it could simply be that the fellow was in a hurry and didn't notice what he did. Couldn't it?"

Ariel and Mrs. Merriweather spoke together.

"No!"

"But why not?"

Ariel and Mrs. Merriweather looked at each other. As Lady Farrington had said, there really was no proof. But both women knew, deep inside, that it had been no accident.

"I cannot tell you how I know, Barbara, but I am quite certain it was no accident. I am just grateful that Miss Hawthorne had her wits about her."

Lady Farrington turned to stare at Ariel, and indeed Mrs. Merriweather seemed to study her with particular shrewdness as well, before she said, "You reacted very quickly, Miss Hawthorne. I am quite impressed. I am also rather surprised. I should not have guessed you would do so well in such a situation."

Ariel colored up. "Papa took me places with him," she said, a defensive note in her voice. "And while he spoke with his friends, their children often were left to entertain me. Many of them were boys, and I learned things that Mama was used to say were most unladylike."

"Unladylike but very useful," Mrs. Merriweather said dryly.

"But how did you think to roll like that?" Lady Farrington could not seem to help asking.

Ariel looked at her. "We were visiting in northern Africa once, many years ago. Papa and Mama were talking with the adults and I was playing with our host's son. Someone pushed us both into the street. The boy grabbed me and rolled with me out of harm's way. I remembered that, I suppose, when this happened just now."

"You have had a very useful education," Mrs. Merriweather repeated, after she had stared at Ariel for another long moment, "and I am very grateful for it. I think, however, that we shall not tell the colonel. He might decide that we ought to curtail our activities even further."

Lady Farrington stared at both of them with a look of impatience in her eyes. "You do not mean to tell me what is going on, do you?" she said.

Mrs. Merriweather regarded her calmly. "No, Barbara," she said, "I do not. Two of us in danger is quite enough. You are to stay completely out of this. And do not tell the colonel, or I shall tell your husband a tale or two he still does not know about the days when I was your governess!"

Lady Farrington, who had been quite clearly about to argue, abruptly closed her mouth. With ill grace she said, "Oh, very well, Miss Tibbles. But when this is over, I shall expect you to tell me everything."

Mrs. Merriweather smiled an innocent smile. "Of course we will, my dear. Of course we will."

She fooled no one. Ariel already knew her well enough to guess that she would tell this lady, and everyone else, precisely as much as she wished them to know and not a word more. Clearly Lady Farrington knew Mrs. Merriweather at least as well as Ariel did, for she frowned with great annoyance but did not even bother to protest.

"Come, Miss Hawthorne," Mrs. Merriweather said, rising to her feet. "It is time for us to go home. The colonel will be wondering what has happened to us."

"Be careful this time going out to your carriage," Lady Farrington said, rising to her feet as well. "Indeed, I think I shall escort you out there. An extra pair of eyes might be useful."

It was a measure of how shaken the former governess must have been that she did not argue. Instead she nodded curtly and said, "Perhaps it would be wise, after all."

But they reached their carriage without the least hint of trouble this time. They were soon handed in, directions given to the coachman, and the door shut. Only when the carriage pulled away from the curb, however, did Mrs. Merriweather allow herself the luxury of giving way to her feelings.

She leaned back against the squabs and closed her eyes. To Ariel she said, eyes still closed, "I really am too old for this. I wish people would stop doing such horrible things."

Ariel leaned forward. In a low, concerned voice she said, "Are you all right, Mrs. Merriweather?"

The former governess's eyes snapped open and she abruptly sat upright. "I am fine," she retorted impatiently. "I just gave way to a moment's megrims. But I am fine. And I am not going to let this stop me. If the fellow who pushed us thought that it would, he will soon find out that he is mistaken!"

And to that, Ariel had nothing to say because Mrs. Merriweather's determination only mirrored her own. She did, however, comment, "I am glad you told the coachman to take us to my father's house. There were far too many people interested in Papa's papers last night. I should like to go through them again."

Mrs. Merriweather nodded. "I rather thought you would. The colonel told me what he overheard. I should like to go through your father's papers, as well. I shall be most curious to see what we might find."

# 16

In another part of town, three men sat in Thornsby's office. Thornsby, Stanfield, and Merriweather all stared at one another. None of them looked entirely at ease. It was Stanfield who broke the ice, so to speak.

"It is absurd to continue to act independently when we could accomplish a great deal more by being allies," the captain said. To Thornsby he added, "I know we are supposed to be sworn to secrecy, but circumstances have made that impossible. We ought to make the best of things and turn them to our advantage. I, for one, am very glad to know that Colonel Merriweather can be depended upon, should we manage to entrap the thieves."

"Thank you, Stanfield," Colonel Merriweather said dryly. "And I find, after the events of the past few days, including two murders, that I quite agree. Do you know," he addressed Thornsby, "whether anyone has shown a particular interest in museum artifacts? Other than scholars, of course?"

"A number of people," Thornsby said grimly, "have been heard to oppose the public acquisition of new exhibits for the museum. Some of them are trying, as they see it, to be fiscally prudent on behalf of the nation. Others, we believe, simply do not want competition for their own extensive collections of artifacts. We are trying to narrow down the list, but so far it is extremely difficult to do so."

"Do you know of someone named Kinkaid?" Merriweather asked.

Thornsby nodded. "He is on our list. He is a well-known collector who takes pride in showing off his collection. It is rumored that he has a private collection, as well, that far exceeds in scope and merit his public one. But since it is private, we have not had a chance to verify the truth of that rumor. He is apparently very selective as to whom he is willing to show his private treasures. Why do you ask?"

"He was at Lady Jersey's last night and claimed friendship with Hawthorne. Offered to help go through his papers. Even warned m'wife to encourage Miss Hawthorne to leave London for a bit," Merriweather explained grimly. "So I wondered."

"Kinkaid is a favorite of Prinny's," Captain Stanfield said slowly. "I suppose this means that no one would dare press him on this or any other matter?"

Thornsby nodded. Colonel Merriweather took up the thread. "So it is up to us, then, to find the kind of proof we would need to put a stop to Kinkaid, if he has had a hand in the thefts at the museum."

"And remember," Thornsby warned, "that we are not certain he has. In the past, so far as we know, he has seemed quite content to merely outbid other collectors for what he wishes to have."

"If he is behind this, we shall find out," Stanfield said with the certainty of youth.

"If he is, we shall do our best to discover proof," Merriweather added with the caution of age. "Someone I know will look into who is creating the false artifacts substituted for the stolen ones. That may help as well."

Thornsby nodded again. "I depend upon you both and have complete confidence that you shall do so. Keep me informed—and be careful," he added. "Anyone who has already killed twice is not likely to hesitate to kill once or twice more."

The two men nodded. "We both have reason," Stanfield said soberly, "to wish to come safely through this affair."

Startled, Thornsby peered at him more closely. "You have never said so before."

Stanfield met his superior's gaze. In a calm and steady voice he said, "I have never had reason to say so before. This time I do."

"Well, I am not displeased to hear it," Thornsby admitted heavily. "In the past, if you have had one flaw, it was that I thought you too reckless. I shall be delighted if that truly has changed. Well, if there is nothing more, gentlemen, you may leave."

Captain Stanfield and Colonel Merriweather rose to their feet and quietly left the building. Once outside they paused. "Where to now?" the captain asked. "The museum?"

Merriweather shook his head. "Call it a hunch," he said. "Between what was said to me and to Mrs. Merriweather and to Miss Hawthorne last night at Lady Jersey's party, it seems there is a great deal of interest in Hawthorne's papers. And not the ones, I should guess, still at the museum, since someone went through Hawthorne's office the day he died. It may be that something other than his scholarly work is at issue here. And if so, he may have kept those particular papers at home. After all, it was there that you and my wife and Miss Hawthorne routed a thief the day of Hawthorne's death. I cannot think it likely that it was a coincidence."

The Dearborns were still at Hawthorne's house and they both exclaimed sharply at Ariel and Mrs. Merriweather's appearance. This did not please the former governess.

"Yes, yes," she said. "Our gowns are past repair, I know. But that is unimportant. Miss Hawthorne and I need to work in her father's library and we do not wish to be disturbed."

"Not even if callers come?" Mrs. Dearborn asked doubtfully.

"Have there been many callers?" Ariel asked.

"Some. Most persistent, some of them be. But I send them to the rightabout quick enough, I promise you. Tells them, I do, the miss ain't home and not likely to be for some time."

"Thank you," Ariel said.

"Can you tell us what they look like?" Mrs. Merriweather asked.

Dearborn gave as good a description as he could, but it was one that might have applied to any number of gentlemen in London. With a tiny sigh, Ariel and Mrs. Merriweather gave it up as hopeless and went into the library.

"We do not wish to be disturbed," Mrs. Merriweather repeated. "Miss Hawthorne is not at home to callers, no matter who they may be."

It was Mrs. Dearborn who replied, "Yes, ma'am. You may depend upon us."

And so Ariel and Mrs. Merriweather found themselves free to go through her father's desk in the library. They tried to work quickly, though they were not at all certain what it was they were looking for.

"I wonder," Ariel said when she paused for a moment, "what Colonel Merriweather and Captain Stanfield will make of the attack upon us this morning."

Mrs. Merriweather turned a horrified look upon her. "I thought we were agreed not to tell them."

Ariel frowned. "Yes, but I have been thinking. Should we not put them on their guard?" she asked.

It was a sensible question. Mrs. Merriweather knew only too well that it was a sensible one. But she shifted uncomfortably and refused to meet Ariel's eyes. "They would only worry, far too much, I assure you, and attempt to curtail our quite natural wish to be involved in the investigation," the former governess said airily. "It is for their own good, and ours, that we do not tell them."

Ariel did not argue any further, but privately she made

her own decision. She would not betray Mrs. Merriweather to the colonel, but the moment she had a chance to speak to Captain Stanfield alone, she would tell him everything. Someone must put the men on their guard, after all. What if some harm should come to either of them because she did not?

The opportunity came far sooner than she expected, for scarcely had she finished making this resolve than the door to the library opened. Both ladies turned to chastise the Dearborns for allowing visitors but stopped as they realized it was Colonel Merriweather and Captain Stanfield who were standing in the open doorway.

"Marian?" the colonel asked, a warning in his voice.

"Miss Hawthorne! What are you and Mrs. Merriweather doing here?" Captain Stanfield demanded. "Do neither of you realize how dangerous it might be?"

Ariel hesitated, not quite certain how to answer. Mrs. Merriweather, however, got a gleam in her eye, and she advanced upon the two men. "What are you doing here? That is what I should like to know!" she countered. "Were you trying to steal a march upon us?"

Captain Stanfield started to object, but the colonel held up a hand to stop him. Then he crossed his arms over his chest and addressed his wife with admirable calm.

"You know very well, Marian, that you ought not to be here," he said. "You and Miss Hawthorne were supposed to pay a few social calls and then return home. And do not tell me that I did not specify *which* home, for you know very well how I would feel about you placing yourself, and Miss Hawthorne, in the path of danger!"

Captain Stanfield, meanwhile, had been studying both ladies closely. Now he said in a slow, careful voice, "Miss Hawthorne, what happened to you and Mrs. Merriweather?"

Ariel looked at the former governess, shrugged as if to say she had no choice, and then told him. "We think someone tried to kill us this morning."

"What?" The exclamation came from both men.

"What the devil do you mean?" Colonel Merriweather asked grimly when she did not immediately answer.

He looked at his wife, but once again it was Ariel who answered. "As Mrs. Merriweather and I were leaving the home of one of her former charges, someone pushed us both in front of a carriage that was racing down the street."

"Are you all right?" Captain Stanfield demanded, coming over to where she stood and peering down at her face with a searching look.

This time it was Mrs. Merriweather who replied. She did not trouble to hide the exasperation she felt as she said, "Miss Hawthorne is perfectly all right. We are both perfectly all right. Well, except for quite a few bruises," she amended, when the colonel glared at her. "And it might have simply been an accident."

The men quite properly ignored this caveat.

"You were quite right to tell us," Captain Stanfield said to Ariel. "We shall be able to be on our guard now. I am also," he added, lowering his voice, "so very glad that you were not hurt. That neither you, nor Mrs. Merriweather, were hurt," he amended hastily.

"Did you see what the person who pushed you looked like?" Colonel Merriweather demanded.

Both Ariel and Mrs. Merriweather shook their heads. "There was no time for us to take note of anything, and in any event, he was behind us," Ariel replied.

"Barbara—Lady Farrington—was watching from the window," Mrs. Merriweather added with a frown. "But she said she could see nothing of the man's features, either. Barbara thought that he had some sort of hat pulled down over his head, and that he moved a trifle hunched over. But she could not say what his height might be, nor describe any of the features of his face."

"A pity," Colonel Merriweather told her grimly. "I should like very much to speak to the fellow."

"As would I," Captain Stanfield said, still looking at

Ariel. To her, he added, "You needn't worry. I shall make certain that nothing happens to you."

"That is all very well, and I hope you may succeed in doing so, Captain Stanfield," the colonel said in acid tones. "But what I should like to know, Marian, is how the pair of you escaped being hurt worse!"

Ariel colored up at that and said hastily, "Oh, we were very lucky. But the point is that someone tried to push us in front of the carriage and so we must all be on our guard."

"Yes, yes. We will be on our guard," the colonel agreed. "But I repeat, Marian, how did the pair of you escape being hurt any worse?"

Mrs. Merriweather looked at Ariel and then at the colonel. "Do not act as if you think I did something extraordinary," she told him tartly, "for I did not. It was Miss Hawthorne who showed the quickness of wit to grab on to me and roll us both safely to the other side of the street. And now," she said before the two men could say anything more, "you had best excuse us. Miss Hawthorne and I must return to Lady Merriweather's house so that she may change her dress before Captain Stanfield escorts her to his mother's house."

"My mother!" Stanfield exclaimed. "I'd almost forgotten! Miss Hawthorne, perhaps I should accompany you. That way, the moment you are ready, we may be on our way. If, that is, we may borrow your carriage?" he asked the colonel.

"Yes, of course, Stanfield," Merriweather said with a nod. He turned to his wife and added sharply, "And you, Marian, may remain here with me. I am certain the captain will be happy to send the carriage back after he is done with it. And there is a great deal of work to be done here. You may as well help me to do it."

It was, odd as it seemed, a peace offering from the colonel to his wife, and she gratefully accepted. Stanfield escorted Ariel out to the carriage, and soon they were on their way to Lady Merriweather's town house.

"Do you think you will be able to slip upstairs unseen?" Captain Stanfield asked doubtfully.

"I shall certainly try. The last thing I would wish is for the servants or Lady Merriweather to ask questions!" Ariel replied fervently.

It was then that Stanfield realized what was bothering him. "You've lost your spectacles," he said.

Ariel grimaced. "Yes, they came off when we were rolling across the street. They were shattered so badly that there was no point in attempting to retrieve them."

"Yes, but . . ."

"But what?" Ariel prodded him when he stopped.

"You don't seem to have any trouble seeing!" Stanfield said in a burst of words.

Ariel colored up. She looked away and then back at him again. There was more than a little guilt in her voice as she tried to explain.

"When Papa first took me to the museum with him, no one wished to have me there. No matter how soberly I dressed, they thought me a frivolous creature, a nuisance and nothing more. And then, one day, I chanced to put Papa's spectacles upon my nose. I meant it just as a lark, you see. But then I found that people treated me differently when I wore the spectacles. Almost as if they could believe I did know something of what they were talking about. And so Papa and I hit upon the notion of having spectacles made for me that had clear glass in them. That way they did not interfere with my eyes but gave me the serious look that was needed."

Stanfield stared at her. After a moment he began to laugh. At her look of indignation, he laughed even harder. "Oh, Miss Hawthorne," he said, "you are a true original. And to think I never guessed they were plain glass, those spectacles you clung to so fervently."

Ariel was spared having to answer, for they were at Lady Merriweather's town house. She managed to slip up the stairs unseen, and Stanfield was left to cool his heels in the drawing room under Lady Merriweather's interested gaze. In the short time he waited for Ariel, that redoubtable lady managed to extract from the captain every pertinent detail as to his breeding, income, and future prospects. She was, he thought, more persuasive and skilled than any military agent he had ever known.

William might have wished himself elsewhere, particularly since the ordeal with his mother lay ahead. But still he stared almost in awe when Miss Hawthorne reappeared dressed in a gown of dark green silk that seemed to swirl about her as she walked and showed off her figure to great advantage. Her hair was piled upon her head in a most becoming way, and she carried the most fetching bonnet he had ever seen. She looked remarkably different, he thought, than she had such a short time before!

Indeed, so awed was he, that William almost forgot to rise to his feet to greet her. A glare from Lady Merriweather brought him to his senses, and he hastily stood and bowed.

"Are you ready, Miss Hawthorne?" he managed to ask.

She nodded and put on her bonnet. Then he offered her his arm and she took it with another smile. William was startled to realize that he found himself trying to think of even more ways to elicit such a delightful look from her.

It alarmed him even more to realize that it did not alarm him to know that Lady Merriweather was regarding the pair of them with obvious approval. And, to a man who had sworn often and fluently that he never meant to marry, those looks should have sent him flying as far away as fast as possible!

With an effort, Stanfield reined in his thoughts. He was quiet as he handed Miss Hawthorne into the carriage and gave his mother's direction to the coachman. It was imperative, he told himself, that he muster a clear head before they arrived at his mother's house. It would not do to feed her matchmaking plans any further!

Miss Hawthorne touched his arm. "You seem distracted," she said. "Are you upset that your mother invited me to come see her today? Ought I to have cried off? It is not too late, if that is what you wish me to do."

William could hear the concern in her voice, and he immediately tried to reassure her. "No," he said, smiling as warmly as he could. "If you had tried to cry off, my mother would simply have found another means to get you alone so that she could get to know you better. Once she has a notion in her head, it is pointless to try to dissuade her."

Miss Hawthorne frowned. "But she seems determined to believe that you and I—"

She broke off, clearly too embarrassed to say bluntly what she meant. William took her hand in his. "If you mean that my mother is matchmaking and wishes to see if you and I have an understanding, you are correct."

"Y-you don't mind that she thinks that?" Miss Hawthorne asked.

William hesitated. He did, of course. But he could not say so. Not when Miss Hawthorne was looking at him with such distress in her eyes.

"My mother," he said slowly, "has been matchmaking for me for years. She will not accept that I do not wish to be married. This way she will focus her plans on you, and I know that I can count on your common sense to prevent you from being taken in by her schemes."

"Oh. I see. Yes, of course I shan't be taken in," Miss Hawthorne replied.

Her voice sounded a little odd to William, but he had no time to ponder the matter, for the carriage was drawing to a halt in front of his mother's town house. For all his brave words, when he saw the way his mother looked at Miss Hawthorne, Captain Stanfield felt a premonition of disaster. It was a premonition that only grew stronger when William realized his two married sisters were waiting in the drawing room to greet Miss Hawthorne as well.

# 17

"Come in and sit down, my dear," Lady Chadbourne said as she led Ariel into the drawing room.

"Thank you, Lady Chadbourne."

"Have you met my daughters? They are Lady Garrick and Lady Toland."

Two ladies who bore a distinct resemblance to both their mother and Captain Stanfield, greeted Ariel with avid interest. Indeed, she had to fight the impulse to turn and flee the room. She looked to Stanfield for support, and he smiled weakly, as though sympathizing with her sense of feeling overwhelmed. Unaccountably, that was enough to raise her spirits sufficiently so that she could greet the ladies with at least a semblance of equanimity.

She smiled. At least she thought she smiled. Certainly she managed to say something that sounded proper because Stanfield's sisters also began to smile. Then they turned to their brother and invited him to sit down next to Ariel.

For a moment, she thought she saw a hint of panic in his eyes, and felt a corresponding panic in her own breast. But then he bowed and came forward and sat carelessly on the sofa beside her, as though it mattered not one whit to him what his mother or his sisters thought.

To Ariel's surprise, they stared at Captain Stanfield's injured arm and seemed to share some private jest.

"You are wearing the sling," Lady Garrick said to him.

"The one we embroidered for you," Lady Toland added.

"Yes."

One word, spoken as though Captain Stanfield was holding on to his temper only with great effort.

Lady Garrick turned to Ariel. "You must understand, Miss Hawthorne," she said. "There was a time when he threatened to burn the thing."

"He swore he would never forgive us for choosing flowers," Lady Toland told her with a grin.

Apparently Ariel's bewilderment showed upon her face, for Lady Chadbourne took pity on her and explained. "When William first came back to us, after he was injured, he seemed to care about nothing and no one. No matter what we said or did, he simply lay there, convinced he would never recover and his future was pointless."

"So they embroidered flowers on my sling," Captain Stanfield said. He smiled as he remembered. "They embroidered the flowers all over my sling. They wished, you see, to provoke me into a rage."

Both his sisters laughed, completely unabashed. "And it worked," Lady Garrick told Ariel.

"It was the most beautiful rage you ever saw," Lady Toland said with a smile.

"And it pulled him out of his decline," Lady Chadbourne concluded.

"So it did," Captain Stanfield agreed. "And that is why I kept it."

"A good thing, too," his mother said tartly, "given how often you seem to injure yourself all over again."

Captain Stanfield stopped smiling. "We are boring Miss Hawthorne with our family stories," he said through gritted teeth.

That turned their attention back to Ariel. The three ladies smiled at her again, and she felt much like she supposed a fox must feel to discover itself being hunted by hounds. She tried to smile back.

"Do you do embroidery, Miss Hawthorne?" Lady Garrick asked.

This was safe ground, Ariel thought with relief. She pulled a handkerchief out of her reticule. "I embroider this flower on all my handkerchiefs," she replied.

"Why, how unusual," Lady Chadbourne said. "I have never seen such an unique flower."

"It is one I saw on my travels with my father," Ariel explained.

"Well, I think it is delightful," Lady Garrick pronounced approvingly.

"Perhaps you can teach us how to do it," Lady Toland suggested.

This, however, was too much for Captain Stanfield. "You presume too much upon my very slight acquaintance with Miss Hawthorne," he told his sisters, all but growling.

They all but purred in reply. Particularly Lady Garrick, who leaned forward and said to Ariel, "We would very much like to hear about your *very slight acquaintance* with our brother."

"Yes," Lady Toland added. "For example, how did you meet?"

"I worked with my father for many years at the museum. Captain Stanfield was helping him to catalog some artifacts from the war, so of course we met," Ariel answered, careful not to explain anything further about their acquaintance.

The ladies took pity on Ariel and forbore, at least for the moment, to press the issue any further. Instead, Lady Toland asked, without once pausing to take a breath, "In what way did you help your father and may I say how sorry we are for your loss?"

"I took notes for him on the artifacts that he and Captain Stanfield and Colonel Merriweather were sorting out," Ariel explained. "I've often done so in the past. And I used to help my father arrange such objects for display," Ariel answered, aware that something

about her answer did not entirely please the other
ladies.

"But now that your father is dead, you will cease
working at the museum, surely?" Lady Chadbourne
asked, a hint of doubt in her voice.

"I suppose I shall have to do so," Ariel answered honestly. "Though I wish it could be otherwise. I love working at the museum."

"But don't you wish to be going to balls instead? Pay-
ing calls upon friends? Driving in the park in the afternoon?" Lady Toland asked with a worried frown.

"No."

"Not at all?" Lady Garrick persisted.

Ariel hesitated. For the briefest of moments she let
herself imagine what it might have been like if her life
had been full of balls and drives in the park and after-
noons with friends. And there was no denying there was
a tug on her heartstrings that she had never known such
a life.

But give up her beloved museum? Allow such pursuits
to replace the intense satisfaction of discussing with her
father this artifact or that one? Forget hours happily
spent poring over books and letters and old records to
track down the provenance of something sent as a present to the museum? No, nothing these ladies spoke of
could possible prove as satisfying as the work she had
shared with her father.

Ariel said so aloud, knowing she was sinking herself
beneath reproach by doing so. To her surprise, Lady
Chadbourne, Stanfield's mother, came to her rescue.

"Do you know, your father was just such a person,"
Lady Chadbourne said to Stanfield. "He, too, preferred
his books to parties and such. The only reason I could
get him to come to London was that the museum was
here. And so were the talks given by the various learned
societies to which he belonged."

She paused and turned back to Ariel. "Yes, Miss Hawthorne, I can understand why you would be loath to give
up such pursuits," she said. "But couldn't you do the

intellectual work you clearly love and still find time to attend some balls and parties and visit friends? Not at once, of course, for I do see that it would not be proper while you are in mourning for your father! But later, perhaps, you might find that such things were not entirely anathema to you?"

It was said coaxingly, and Ariel found she was not proof against Lady Chadbourne's charm. "P-perhaps I might," she agreed.

"There. You see? We have something in common, after all," Lady Chadbourne said with approval.

"Mother!"

She turned to look at her son. "What is it, dear? I thought you would be happy that your sisters and I like Miss Hawthorne."

"I am," he said through what sounded like clenched teeth. "But I fear you are making her uncomfortable."

"Nonsense," Lady Chadbourne retorted. She turned to Ariel. "We are not making you uncomfortable, are we?"

She ought to have said that of course they were not. She knew that was what she ought to say. But Ariel didn't. Instead she once more chose honesty.

"I must confess," Ariel said, directing a level gaze upon her hostess, "that I do not quite understand why you invited me here. To inspect me, I presume, but I do not entirely understand why."

Well, that was plain speaking! Beside her, Ariel could feel Stanfield stiffen. Was he distressed with her? All at once she wished the words could be taken back. But then she realized he was laughing.

"There, Mama! She has put paid to your discreet attempts to interrogate her. Well, what are you going to tell her? Why *are* you so determined to discover everything you can about Miss Hawthorne?" Stanfield asked, sounding far more cheerful than Ariel would have expected.

As Lady Chadbourne bristled, his sister, Lady Garrick, laughed nervously and said, "Really, William, you are embarrassing Miss Hawthorne!"

He looked at her and said in a cool voice, "I thought that was what all of you were doing. Come. Let us have the gloves off. Miss Hawthorne and I have worked together at the museum. I am fond of her company. More than that, I suggest you not imagine. For until there is an announcement, any such thinking would be premature."

His other sister, Lady Toland pounced. "Until? So there *will* be an announcement?" she demanded.

Stanfield sighed. "I did not say so."

His mother leaned forward and patted his hand. It was Ariel, however, to whom she said, "I trust you will forgive us, my dear, for our presumption. It is just that we have never seen William show so much interest in any young lady. And we wish very much for him to be happy. Should your, er, friendship lead to anything more, we would be delighted. If not, well, we have made the acquaintance of a very interesting young woman. I hope you are equally happy to meet us?"

"O-of course, Lady Chadbourne," Ariel replied in a somewhat dazed voice.

"Mama, you are raising expectations!" Stanfield said sternly. "It is most improper of you."

Lady Chadbourne looked at him blandly. "Well, but it is your responsibility to make certain that Miss Hawthorne understands clearly how matters stand. If you had not given us cause to make such an assumption, I assure you, William, that we would not have done so."

Stanfield snorted his disbelief. But his mother merely turned to Ariel and began to talk with her about the work she had done with her father, and by degrees Ariel found herself feeling at ease with Stanfield's family, for as she discovered, their fashionable gowns and elegantly arranged hairstyles hid lively minds that showed an interest far beyond that found among most women of the *ton*. Or perhaps it was only her prejudice that made Ariel think these ladies so unusual. When she stopped to consider the matter, she had to admit that she had insufficient experience to know. It was, she discovered, an interesting realization.

Indeed, when it came time to take her leave of the ladies of Stanfield's family, Ariel found herself oddly reluctant to do so. And when they promised to call upon her soon, she found herself actually looking forward to such a thing.

Outside, Stanfield let out a deep breath and apologized yet again. "I am very sorry. I ought to have known, indeed, I did know how outrageous my mother and sisters could and were likely to be. Perhaps I should have warned you. I hope they did not make you too uncomfortable?"

He sounded almost anxious to hear her answer, and Ariel laughed. "To the contrary," she said. "I have always wondered what it would be like to have my mama still alive. And what it would be like to have had sisters. Now I have some sense of the matter. I've no doubt sisters would have rubbed me the wrong way a hundred times a day, and yet, at the same time, I find myself wishing I had some."

Stanfield smiled. "Yes, you've hit it off just so. I adore my sisters, and yet I should be glad to strangle them at least once every time we are together. Their tendency to matchmake is the worst of it."

"They are only concerned for your happiness," Ariel said shyly. "I am flattered to think that perhaps they would be happy if you took that sort of interest in me— even if it is nonsense."

Stanfield paused to hand her into the carriage, and he was silent as he climbed in after. Only when they were moving did he speak, and his voice was a trifle husky as he said, "Is it such an absurd notion? That I might take an interest in you? Or you in me?"

Did he mean what he seemed to be saying? But what about his words on the way to Lady Chadbourne's house? The ones where he said he knew he could count on her common sense to keep her from being taken in by his mother's schemes? Did he, perhaps, not even know his own mind? Captain Stanfield was waiting for her answer and somehow she had to manage some sort of reply. She took a deep breath.

"N-no," Ariel admitted, her own voice a trifle shaky. "It is n-not an entirely absurd notion, I suppose."

He took her hand then and raised it to his lips, where he kissed her at the wrist. "Well, I do not think it absurd at all," Stanfield told her.

Then, giving her time to draw back if she wished, he touched the side of her cheek and then cupped her chin with his hand, drawing her face closer to his.

She ought to draw back, Ariel told herself. But she could not. Instead, all she could do was watch with fascination as his head descended toward hers. And when he kissed her, she let out a tiny sigh at the realization of how long she had dreamed of such a moment.

It was a gentle kiss, so soft she might almost have imagined it. But the second kiss was no fantasy. Nor was it nearly so gentle. Instead it seemed almost to be a way of claiming her, of making certain she would not soon forget the feel of his lips upon hers, or the taste of him either.

Somehow her arms seemed to wind themselves about his neck just as his good arm pulled her up against him. Every moment seemed more improper than the one before. But heaven help her, Ariel could not protest. Not when her soul cried out for even more.

All too soon, it seemed, the carriage drew to a halt again. Ariel and Stanfield hastily sprang apart, and she touched her hair to make certain it was not too badly disarranged. He watched as she settled her bonnet once more securely upon her head. And then it was time to climb out of the carriage, pretending to take no more than the most civil of farewells to Captain Stanfield. Did she deceive the footman who opened the carriage door? Or Lady Merriweather's majordomo when he held the front door of the town house open for her? Ariel did not think so, but her own thoughts were in far too much disarray for her to greatly care.

What was she to do? Not for the first time, Ariel desperately wished that she still had a mother to turn to for advice. Fortunately Mrs. Merriweather was waiting for her. The older woman took one look at her face and began to shepherd her to a small parlor, rather than the drawing room from which voices floated out to them.

"You will not wish to encounter company just now," Mrs. Merriweather observed briskly. "Nor will they expect you to do so. Come, we may be perfectly private in here."

When Ariel was settled in a chair, Mrs. Merriweather looked at her kindly but merely chose to wait. In the end, it was Ariel who made the decision to confide in her, without the need for any coaching to do so.

She told the former governess all about the afternoon, even confiding that Stanfield had kissed her in the carriage. Far from being shocked, the older woman nodded approvingly. "So he is discovering that his sentiments march in tune with yours? Excellent!"

"But Mrs. Merriweather, wasn't it most improper for Captain Stanfield to kiss me in such a way?" Ariel could not help but protest.

The older woman smiled. "Well, yes. And ordinarily, if I were your governess, for example, I should be scolding you for allowing such familiarity before an offer had been made. But these are not, I think, ordinary circumstances. Nothing would delight me more than to see you happily settled. But I will admit a kiss promises nothing of the sort. And I should not like to see any man give you a slip upon the shoulder. So you had best not be alone with him again. Nor allow such an embrace again, at least not unless and until he offers for you. But once? Well, under the circumstances I think it a most promising sign."

More bewildered than ever, Ariel fled to her room. Had the whole world gone mad? More important, had she?

# 18

Days passed, and Ariel felt a growing frustration. All work on the artifacts had come to a halt by decree of the museum trustees. They did not, they said, wish any more work to be done until a replacement had been found for Mr. Hawthorne. Nothing had been found among her father's papers to explain why so many people were interested in them. Perhaps, she told herself, they really were simply interested in his research.

On this particular morning, Ariel stared out the window at the rain. It matched her mood to perfection, and she could not be sorry for the fact that it would keep callers from coming to Lady Merriweather's house. If she could not go to the museum, at least she was not forced to endure the condolences of people who had never known her father and who would, if given half a chance, tell her that her own pursuits were most improper.

No, she could not regret anything that kept the gossips of the *ton* at home. Ariel was tired of being stared at as if she were an exhibit from some show of oddities.

Mrs. Merriweather's sympathetic voice came from behind Ariel. "A horrible day, isn't it?"

She turned to smile wistfully at the older woman. "One becomes accustomed to such weather. I was just thinking that at least it would keep away callers. And how I could only feel grateful for that."

Mrs. Merriweather squeezed Ariel's shoulder reassuringly. "It has been hard for you, I know. And I can well understand how you feel. I, on the other hand, must deplore such a horrid sight, when I know that I shall be going out in it later."

Ariel was too polite to ask where she meant to go, but the colonel's wife told her anyway. "I have consented to go to a ball this evening with Lady Merriweather. She has brought it to my attention that I risk offending too many important people if I continue to refuse all the invitations that are sent to me. And, in any event, the Duchess of Berenford was once one of my charges. She is Lady Farrington's sister."

Ariel smiled at the older woman. She knew her very well by now. "No doubt you also hope to discover something useful while you are there?" she hazarded shrewdly.

Mrs. Merriweather's eyes narrowed, and for a moment she did not look pleased. But then she nodded approvingly. "I've said you have your wits about you. You are right, of course. I do hope to learn something useful. If, as the colonel suspects, a member of the *ton* is behind the thefts at the museum, I may hear something of use if I sit with the tattle boxes and toss out a useful tidbit or two myself."

Ariel shook her head. "No wonder you were such a formidable governess!" she said. "I shudder to think what it would have been like for any poor girl trying to outwit you!"

Mrs. Merriweather drew herself up to her full height and sniffed disdainfully. "I should hope the girls I had charge of had the wit to realize how pointless it would be and did not do so more than once."

Ariel laughed, not in the least deceived by the air of reproof. "Confess," she said. "You enjoyed matching wits with your charges and would have been sadly disappointed had they lacked the strength of character to try!"

"Well, perhaps," Mrs. Merriweather conceded. "So long as they did realize in the end that I had their best interests in mind."

They both grinned at each other, but then Mrs. Merriweather reached out and put a hand on Ariel's arm. "I cannot help but think this is a difficult time for you, my dear. Do you mind being left alone this evening while we go to the ball? If you wish, I could stay home with you."

Ariel was touched by the other woman's kindness, and yet, if anything, she felt too hemmed about with the kindness and concern that led the others to keep such a close eye upon her. But of course she could not say so. Instead, Ariel smiled and replied, "Please go to the ball. I would like to think of you having fun or, at any rate, discovering something that might tell us who was behind the thefts at the museum and perhaps even my father's and Tom's deaths."

Mrs. Merriweather dropped her hand from Ariel's arm and nodded. "I do think your father would have approved. He would have wanted us, I think, to find the answers—if not for himself, then for Tom."

She paused, and a bleak look came into her eyes. "That poor simple young man," Mrs. Merriweather said. "His death still haunts me. They must have known he could do them very little harm. And it positively infuriates me that the museum trustees are willing to pay Bow Street to find your father's killer but will not spend a penny to find Tom's. To be sure, the colonel has offered to pay Mr. Collins to find Tom's killer since the trustees have taken over the cost for your father, and in any event, the two person's responsible may be one and the same, but it still rankles."

"And you care, even though Tom was a stranger to you," Ariel said.

"For twenty years I was a governess," Mrs. Merriweather said quietly. "And for twenty years I knew my place. But I never forgot that once I had been a young lady, too. That had my father not died penniless I might have married well and been one of the ones who hired women like me. And for twenty years, there was not a day that went by when someone did not make clear to me how unimportant they thought I was. How little someone in my position was valued."

"Except the families who employed you," Ariel countered gently.

Mrs. Merriweather nodded. "I was fortunate. By the time I was called in, the families were so desperate for someone to bring their daughters to heel that they would not have dared do something so foolish as to snub me. But there were always others. Sometimes they were other servants. Sometimes it was visitors to the house or the more distantly related connections. But one way or another, I was never allowed to forget that I was not as valued or important to society as the families who hired me. So I feel, in many ways, very much like poor Tom, and when they say his life did not matter, it is as though they say the same of mine."

Just at that moment a maid came into the room, a somewhat frantic look upon her face. "Mrs. Merriweather? Nurse asks that you come upstairs at once! It seems your daughter is, er, being difficult."

With a sigh, the older woman left the room, and Ariel, curious to see the child of a former governess, indeed the child of *this* particular former governess, followed. Surely the child of the infamous Miss Tibbles ought to be a paragon of virtues? Prettily behaved and clever and well educated? Somehow, it did not sound as if this was precisely the case.

Upstairs, a rather harried-looking older woman greeted Mrs. Merriweather at the door to the nursery. "You must speak to your daughter, ma'am," Nurse said firmly. "She won't listen to a word I say."

Mrs. Merriweather advanced into the nursery. "Elizabeth!"

A little girl with bright lively eyes looked up at her mother. In the calmest of voices she said, "Yes, Mama?"

"What have you been doing now?"

"Decorating the nursery, Mama. It needed decorating," the winsome child replied with wide, innocent eyes.

The nurse muttered something about devil's spawn. The maid whispered to Ariel, most improperly, that the

child was a real terror and none of them wanted the task
of feeding or bathing her.

Mrs. Merriweather looked around at the splashes of
paint that now covered the walls and tables and said,
"To be sure, it brightens up the room, Elizabeth, but this
is not our house and it is not your place to decorate.
They might like it drab and dingy in here."

The nurse gasped in outrage. Ariel had to smother a
giggle of amusement. The maid listened avidly, and there
was no doubt she meant to regale the staff below stairs
with a vivid description of all that was taking place.

The child merely looked at her mother and set down
the paint. She put her now brightly stained hands behind
her back. "Yes, Mama," she said with a meekness that
deceived no one, not with the evidence of her true nature
so pointedly in front of all of them.

"Someone will need to clean this up," Mrs. Merriweather persisted.

The child stared up at her mother. "I'm too little,"
she said.

"Oh, no, you're not!" Nurse said briskly. To the maid
she added, "Go fetch cloths and hot water. Miss Merriweather is going to be very busy over the next few
hours."

"But I'm hungry," Elizabeth said wistfully.

"And you'll be a good deal hungrier before you're
done," Nurse snapped at her.

"I'll miss my nap?" Elizabeth offered hopefully.

"So you will! Or rather, you'll take it later. Indeed,
now that I think about it, you needn't worry, for you'll
be going to bed far earlier than usual tonight," Nurse
told her roundly, her face deep red with anger.

"Well, perhaps she could . . ."

Mrs. Merriweather didn't get any further than that because the nurse rounded on her. "I'll thank you not to
interfere with my taking care of the child, Mrs. Merriweather. I know what I'm about! You know very well
that mothers are too softhearted to do what ought to be
done with their children."

"Now look here. I was a governess for twenty years," Mrs. Merriweather tried again.

"Yes, and knowing that was so, I can't understand how or why you have done such a poor job with your own child," Nurse retorted. "Now I will thank you to clear out and let me do my job. Elizabeth, you will clean up this mess the moment Betsy returns with the hot water and cloths and you will not eat until you are done."

"Mama?"

It cost Mrs. Merriweather a great deal to answer as she did. Ariel could see the difficulty with which she controlled her temper and her voice. But in the end the former governess looked at her daughter and said sternly, "You will do as Nurse tells you."

"Yes, Mama."

The child's expression was mulish, and Ariel would not have taken bets that she would behave once they were gone. Nonetheless, she found the entire exchange vastly educational as well as entertaining. Apparently Mrs. Merriweather realized that she did so, for she turned to Ariel and snapped at her sharply. "Well? Come along! We aren't needed here to distract my daughter! Indeed, I cannot think what you are doing here at all."

"Yes, Mrs. Merriweather," Ariel said meekly. "I was just curious. I have not much been around children, you see. I thought to learn a little of what they are like. And I was curious to see how one ought to raise a child."

Mrs. Merriweather glared at Ariel, as though suspecting the younger woman was roasting her. But apparently she read nothing but honesty in Ariel's eyes because after a moment she relented. Indeed, even her shoulders seem to lose a little of their stiffness.

"Yes, well, I suppose it is only natural that you should wonder. Particularly as you are of an age, indeed past age, to be thinking of marrying and setting up a nursery of your own. It is not always like that, you understand. It is the strange surroundings here in Lady Merriweather's house that are upsetting my daughter. Naturally, at home she would not dream of behaving in such a manner!"

"Naturally," Ariel murmured in reply.

Again the other woman looked at her sharply and again decided not to take offense. "Yes, well, we were talking of other matters, but I cannot recall what they were."

"Nor can I," Ariel admitted.

Mrs. Merriweather consulted the clock over the fireplace as they entered the drawing room. She clucked her tongue. "This day is passing far too quickly," she complained. "Soon I shall have to go and dress for the ball. I do wish I could dance, instead of having to sit with the tabbies, but I suppose it can't be helped. Oh, well, my dear. When you are again able to go to such things, you must dance enough for both of us."

Ariel would have protested that she did not think she would have so very many opportunities to do so, but Mrs. Merriweather was already moving out of the room and toward the stairs, muttering about stitching up a tiny tear in the flounce of her gown.

And Ariel was once more left alone, a circumstance that suited her perfectly. She went to her own room. Outside, the rain still came down steadily and ran dirty rivulets on the outside of the window glass. She traced one of the rivulets with her finger and wondered if this grief, this emptiness inside her heart since her father's death, would ever go away.

# 19

The colonel and Mrs. Merriweather regarded each other with mutual concern. "You will be careful, Marian, won't you?" he asked, a stern note to his voice. "You do understand that you are not to alarm anyone with your questions? Nor to confront Mr. Kinkaid, or anyone else for that matter, with your suspicions?"

Marian fiddled with the lace at her wrists rather than meet his eyes. This was not the time, she decided, to tell him that she had secreted both a knife and a pistol on her person. Instead, she sniffed and said, "As if I could be in any danger in the midst of a ball! No doubt it will be a dreadfully conventional and boring evening."

"Perhaps," he conceded reluctantly. "But who is to say what might happen after you leave, or the next day, should you ask the wrong questions of the wrong person? My dear, you must promise me that you will be careful!"

She looked at him then, and there was concern in her eyes as she replied, "You must be careful as well, Andrew! You are the one running the risks tonight. Must you stand guard at the museum? Why can you not have the Bow Street Runner, Mr. Collins, do so?"

The colonel sighed. "Collins will be there. But I must be there as well. We must catch these thieves, Marian. If we are fortunate, we will find they are also the ones who killed Mr. Hawthorne."

"And Tom," Marian added.

"Yes, of course, and Tom," the colonel replied impatiently. "But one man cannot do it alone. Therefore the Runner and I shall both go."

"What about Stanfield? Why not take him with you?" Marian persisted. "Would three not be better than two?"

"No doubt," Colonel Merriweather conceded. "But he is to go to the ball tonight and see what he can learn among the gentlemen."

"Why couldn't you do that?" Marian asked. "Then we could dance together," she added coaxingly.

The colonel reached out and pulled her into his arms. "Minx!" he said. "You know very well that I should much prefer to be dancing than hiding out in a dusty corner of the museum. But Stanfield knows these men far better than I do. They are more of an age with him, and he has not been out of society, as I have for so many years. He will have a much better chance of discovering something useful than I ever could. Besides, with his injured arm and leg, he will seem much less of a threat than I would, should anyone begin to suspect him of too great an interest in the wrong things."

"I do not like it," Marian said, drawing back and allowing herself a heavy sigh. "I do not like either of you placing yourselves in the slightest danger."

"But you do not hesitate to do so yourself," the colonel pointed out sternly. "Indeed, if I had my way, you and Elizabeth would be bundled into a carriage and sent straight back home at once! I should never have brought you with me to London. I certainly would not have done so had I had the slightest inkling there could be any danger here. Now, go with my aunt to the ball and enjoy yourself. And remember—if anyone should ask, I am suffering from a touch of the gout and in no fit mood to be seen in company."

"As if you have ever suffered from gout in your life," Marian retorted disdainfully.

"Yes, well, in circumstances such as these, I should far rather our opponents underestimate than overestimate me," he said roundly. "Now, go! My aunt will be downstairs already, and you know how she hates waiting."

Marian turned to go. Over her shoulder, however, she could not resist tossing one last charge at him. "Yes, and I think that is the cruelest thing you have done, both to your aunt and to me, insisting that we spend the evening in each other's company! She may have accepted our marriage, but she has never come to like it—or me."

And with that parting shot, she was gone. The colonel looked after his wife for a very long moment before he drew on his gloves and checked his pistol to make certain it was loaded. He also decided to take with him a rather nasty-looking knife, just in case. The Runner, Collins, had promised to bring rope, enough for each of them to have a length of it, just in case they should be so fortunate as to catch the thieves tonight.

Then he waited. The colonel had no wish to encounter his aunt, or to have Marian plead her cause one more time, before they left. Only when he was certain they must be well on their way, did he go downstairs and out the front door. He was pleased to note that the rain had stopped.

The Duchess of Berenford's ball was crowded, which was not in the least surprising, for she was a noted hostess and there were few people who would turn down an invitation from her. Even the weather had cooperated, turning fine just in time for guests to depart for the ball.

This was all to the good, Captain Stanfield thought. It meant there would be a great many gentlemen hiding out from the ladies in the card rooms. And a great many conversations to surreptitiously listen in on. One could toss out a question and let others carry the conversation, and if it didn't prove promising, one could move on without being noticed.

It would also, he told himself, be useful to be seen in conversation with several young ladies. It was amazing how much they sometimes knew and would tell about their families without realizing they ought not to do so. Anyone seeing him would simply assume that he was trying to throw his mama off the scent! After the other night, at Lady Jersey's house, he knew bets had been placed at White's as to whether he was finally going to succumb to the parson's mousetrap and marry the notorious bluestocking, Miss Hawthorne. No one would wonder at his desire to put paid to such speculation by speaking with as many young ladies as possible.

As he bowed to yet another dowager, William noted that Mrs. Merriweather and the colonel's aunt had just come into the ballroom. He had no doubt she also meant to make her own inquiries, but that would be among the older ladies of the *ton*. Well, that was all to the good. They would certainly tell her things he could not possibly ask without arousing just the sort of speculation he most wished to avoid. The colonel, he knew, would be at the museum, if not at this very moment, then soon. And he thought that a very good thing as well.

"Ah, Stanfield, my boy!" a hearty voice said nearby.

William turned to see Lord Lowell surrounded by a circle of friends. "Lord Lowell!" he said with genuine pleasure. "How are you?"

"I am in excellent health. Come join the group of us in a game of cards. I want to hear all about the museum and the goings-on there. I've heard that you knew the man who was killed."

Since this accorded well with William's own plans, he was happy to agree. In any event, Lord Lowell had been a good friend to his father, and he always enjoyed the man's company. One card game led to another, and conversations swirled all around. William didn't even have to try to bring any of the conversations around to the subject of the museum because Lord Lowell did so for him.

"Tell us, my boy, about the death of Mr. Hawthorne. Shocking thing. Positively shocking! They say he was stabbed. Were you there?"

"I arrived that morning at the museum after he was killed," William replied.

"Any notion who did it?" another gentleman asked.

"I wish I knew," William said with perfect honesty. "But I've no more notion than anyone else."

"Any notion the reason it happened?" a third gentleman put in.

William shrugged. "Who knows? I might think it was scholarly rivalry, but I cannot imagine two scholars fighting—at least not physically."

"Could someone have been stealing from the museum?" yet another voice asked.

Startled, Stanfield looked up to see a gentleman standing beside the card table and regarding him with hooded eyes. Kinkaid. He wondered if he was being baited. William chose his words with great care.

"I suppose it is possible," he said slowly. "But what would anyone wish to steal? There is some gold and jewelry at the museum, to be sure, but so recognizable, I would think, as to make such a theft pointless."

"Not if the person wished to melt it down for the gold and sell the stones separately," Lord Lowell pointed out thoughtfully. "Is that what you meant, Kinkaid?"

Kinkaid shook his head. "No. I was thinking more in terms of artifacts."

That brought a guffaw from one of the gentlemen seated at the table. Unperturbed, Kinkaid said, "You may think it absurd, sir, but I assure you that there are those of us willing to pay a great deal for the sorts of things to be found in that museum."

"And did *you* pay for some of the sorts of things to be found in the museum?" a fellow bolder than Stanfield asked sarcastically.

From those who knew Kinkaid well, there was a stunned silence. He, however, chose to be amused. "No, Birkett, I did not pay to have things stolen from the museum, if that is what you are asking. Nor did I arrange to have Hawthorne killed. I confess, however, to an avid curiosity as to who did. A curiosity, I would guess, that is shared by young Captain Stanfield. Particularly in light of his interest in Miss Hawthorne."

William flushed. He decided to brazen it out. "Of

course I should like to know who killed Hawthorne," he agreed lightly. "And yes, I should like to know for Miss Hawthorne's sake as well as for my own. But I'm no Bow Street Runner! I've no notion who could have done such a thing."

Still Kinkaid stared at Stanfield, and it was as though he could read the younger man's mind. He leaned forward as he said, "I did not have a hand in this, and I would give much to know who did. If I can be of assistance, please do not hesitate to call on me for help."

William could only nod, unnerved by the encounter. What the devil did it mean? Before he could gather his wits sufficiently to think of something else to say, Kinkaid waved a careless hand at the group and moved away, leaving Stanfield more confused than ever. The others made jests about Kinkaid's eccentricity, for which William was grateful in that it covered his own silence.

In another part of the ballroom, Marian Merriweather suppressed yet another sigh. Really, listening to the latest *on dits* was surprisingly tiresome! If only she could simply ask the questions she wished to ask. But that would have drawn undue attention to herself and perhaps even put their quarry on alert. She did not need the colonel's warning to know how foolish that would be.

But she listened and hoped that something useful would be spoken. And eventually it was. "Mrs. Merriweather," one of the ladies tittered, "you were at the museum when that man was found dead, weren't you?"

"Yes." She spoke with a chilly reserve, and it answered very well, for the others leaned forward, avid to discuss the matter further.

"Wasn't it a shocking sight? And that poor girl, Miss Hawthorne, forced to see her father dead!"

"I have heard she is staying with you at Lady Merriweather's town house," another chimed in.

"Yes, she is. And Miss Hawthorne is a delightful young lady," Marian said stiffly. "Indeed, she is refreshingly genuine without the slightest trace of nonsense about her."

"Yes, but men like nonsense," still another lady observed dryly.

"Well, of course they do! What man wishes to think his wife's intellect may be greater than his own," one dowager said tartly.

"One may hope that Miss Hawthorne will have the good fortune to find a gentleman who values her as she deserves," Marian said in an austere voice.

"One hears that she already has," the first lady said with a little smile. "Not that I think Lady Chadbourne can be pleased. She, no doubt, has hoped her son would set his sights much higher, for he might very well have done so, even if he is a younger son. But you, Mrs. Merriweather, must know the truth of the matter."

Marian regarded the other lady with a lift of her eyebrows that signaled both disbelief and reproof. It was a look that had served her well all the years she had been a governess, and it did not fail her now.

"I know that nothing has been said, no promises given, and Miss Hawthorne is far too wise to anticipate anything before it occurs," she replied. "In any event, her thoughts are, as they quite properly ought to be, on her father's death right now. She is scarcely thinking of romance when he has been in the ground less than a week."

"Quite a proper young lady, it seems," someone said with a hint of sarcasm in her voice.

Marian turned to stare down the offender. "Indeed she is. One might wish all young ladies of the *ton* were as nicely mannered as Miss Hawthorne."

Since the woman who had spoken had a daughter notorious for her wild streak, this was considered to be a home hit, and the lady retired from the lists, suddenly discovering a need to seek refreshments. In the silence that followed, Marian dared anyone else to speak against Miss Hawthorne. No one took up the challenge.

When she was satisfied they were all properly cowed,

Marian returned to the theme that interested her. "The
museum," she said lightly, "is a fascinating place. Have
any of you visited there?"

And that set the talk going in precisely the direction
she wished. All she had to do now, Marian told herself,
was wait to see what happened and who might know
what.

Lady Merriweather, meanwhile, had her own coterie
of ladies and gentlemen hanging on her every word. It
was an entirely new experience for her. People respected
Lady Merriweather, but she had never found herself so
very much in demand as she did now.

"With your nephew and his wife so involved with the
murders at the museum, you must know details no one
else does," one lady said a trifle breathlessly.

"Indeed, I do," Lady Merriweather agreed.

"How close are they to catching the killer?" asked a
gentleman with exquisite politeness and respect in his
voice.

Lady Merriweather began to feel a trifle uneasy. "I
cannot tell you any details," she said with absolute truth.

"Oh, Lady Merriweather, I am sure you must know
much more than you are saying!" another lady trilled.

"Yes, surely your nephew and his wife confide in you,"
another gentleman chimed in.

She ought to deny it; Lady Merriweather knew she
was foolish to do otherwise. But the looks of admiration
and respect were such balm to her soul. And really, what
harm could there be in prevaricating just a trifle? It was
not as though anyone here could possibly be involved.
So, giving in to temptation, Lady Merriweather nodded.
"Of course I am in my nephew's confidence. He and his
wife tell me everything and you may expect an interesting development very soon. Perhaps as soon as tomorrow
morning. Indeed . . . But, no, I must not say another
word! My lips are sealed," she said.

"Surely you do not think *we* would tell anyone?" yet another lady said, leaning forward.

Lady Merriweather was tempted, so very tempted. And yet there was nothing she could say, even if she wanted to do so. Her gaze caught the eye of a gentleman, and she frowned. Something about him made her distinctly uncomfortable. His eyes went wide. Hastily she looked away and tried to bring the conversation to a close.

"I said I shan't say another word on the subject," she repeated. "My lips are sealed."

When Lady Merriweather looked up again, the gentleman had moved away, and she tried to recall his name. A pity vanity kept her from wearing her spectacles. Perhaps if he hadn't been standing to the back of the group, she would have been able to recognize the gentleman. But as it was, she was simply grateful he was gone.

He was gone from Lady Merriweather's circle, but not from the ball, although he did slip outside to make certain arrangements. Perhaps the old woman was bluffing, but under the circumstances he couldn't afford to take the risk. Not when she talked of interesting developments by tomorrow morning.

A gentleman bowed to Mrs. Merriweather. "May I have this dance?" he asked.

She stared at him. Should she? It would look so foolish, a woman of her age. And this was Mr. Kinkaid! But . . . But she did so dearly love to waltz. And perhaps, Marian told herself, she could learn something useful from him by doing so.

Still, she might have had the strength of character to refuse had she not heard the shocked murmurs around her.

"Mrs. Merriweather? To waltz at *her* age?"

"Why, it would be positively shocking!"

And perhaps that was what did it, for before she knew

what she was about, Marian was on her feet, holding out her hand to Mr. Kinkaid. "I should be delighted," she said.

He grinned a most alarming grin and led her out onto the dance floor. Mr. Kinkaid, whatever his flaws of character might have been, was an excellent dancer. He was also quite capable of carrying on a conversation as he went through the steps.

"So. The famous, or perhaps I should say, infamous Miss Tibbles! What a dragon of a governess you were once reputed to be!"

Marian stiffened at that, and he laughed.

"No, please, I meant no offense," he said hastily. "I am quite in awe of your character and determination. And you are every inch the lady. But I do hope that reputation was accurate and you have succeeded in persuading Miss Hawthorne not to take any foolish risks."

"Foolish risks?" Marian echoed, her mind torn between a desire to learn what she could from Mr. Kinkaid and her enjoyment of the waltz.

Kinkaid gave a sigh of what might have been exasperation. "You are, all of you, far too persistent in asking questions. It could be dangerous."

Marian stiffened. "Are you threatening me, sir?" she demanded.

He stared down at her and replied in the smoothest of voices, "I should never be so foolish, Miss Tibbles. Er, Mrs. Merriweather. I am simply trying to warn you, for your own good. There are, after all, villains in this world."

Her eyes narrowed and her voice was curt as she replied, "Then those *villains* are the ones who had best have a care!"

His lips tightened in disapproval, and Marian had the sinking sensation that Andrew would say she should never have been so blunt. But her temper had gotten the better of her. Still, for the rest of the waltz Mr. Kinkaid was perfectly amiable, and at the end of it he fetched her a glass of champagne.

# 20

Ariel sat alone in the library. With everyone gone, the house felt empty to her. She was reading a novel in the hopes that it might divert, at least for a little while, her thoughts and concerns. It was supposed to be an engaging tale, but Ariel found that it could not hold her interest. What was it to her what some silly creature did when the least common sense would have prevented disaster?

But what else was she to do? She found it hard to simply be alone with her thoughts. Better to pretend to care about silly creatures she would have no use for in real life.

Still, Ariel could not deny that she greeted the appearance of Lady Merriweather's majordomo with something akin to relief. Particularly when he told her there was a message for her. His disapproval was quite evident, even though it went unspoken as he stepped aside to let her see the messenger.

A young boy stepped forward and handed Ariel a folded sheet of paper. "Guv'nor told me to give it to you, if anything 'appened to 'im. Said I were to wait ten days. Weren't to let no one see me give it to you, neither."

This last was said with a glare at Lady Merriweather's servant, who merely sniffed disdainfully in reply. Ariel tried to soothe his ruffled feelings. "I am certain my father did not mean to worry about him," she said.

The boy wiped his nose on his sleeve, and his distress

was evident. " 'e told me no one, no one, were to see. And I would of give it to you at your 'ouse, but you don't never come there no more! Took all me wits to wheedle out where you was from them wots taking care 'o yer 'ouse.''

"You've done the best you could, and my father would be very grateful," Ariel said, trying to reassure the boy but not knowing how. "Perhaps you could have something to eat in the kitchen while I read the letter my father left for me?"

This last was said to Lady Merriweather's servant, who reluctantly nodded. "That could be arranged," he agreed. To the boy he said, "This way."

Completely confused, Ariel waited until they were gone before she unfolded the paper. The words, written in the hand she knew so well, brought tears to her eyes. But she forced them back and began to read whatever it was her father had taken such strange precautions to have delivered to her.

*My dearest Ariel,*

>*If you are reading this message, it means that I am dead. You must go to the museum and look inside our secret hiding place. There you will find something that explains everything. Do not let anyone at the museum know what you are doing, nor the Merriweathers. Not, at any rate, until after you have read what you will find there and decide what you wish to do.*
>
>*Know that I love you, Ariel, and wish it had not come to this.*

>>>*Your loving Papa,*
>>>*Richard Hawthorne*

Ariel stared at the message. She knew what he meant, of course. The second stuffed giraffe at the head of the main stairway. The question was, how was she to get whatever was hidden there without anyone at the museum seeing her or asking questions? For that matter, by morning the Merriweathers would know of the message delivered to her and wish to know what it was about. Papa could not have guessed these would be her circumstances when he arranged to have the letter delivered. He had thought it would be easy for her to do what he wished.

She read the note again. There was urgency not only in his words, but also in the writing itself. Somehow this was terribly important, and she could not ignore what he asked her to do. But how?

Slowly a plan grew in her mind, and Ariel moved with determination to the desk in the library. There was both paper and ink there, she knew. Her decision made, she sat and penned her own note as quickly as she could, then went to give it to the boy in the kitchen.

"Deliver it into Captain Stanfield's hands," she said. "Only his hands. He will be at the Duchess of Berenford's ball tonight. He has one arm in a sling and leans upon a cane. You must wait outside the ball until he leaves it, then insist he read the message at once."

She pressed a few coins into his hand, enough to make his eyes open very wide and cause him to vow fervently that he would do just as she asked. A servant was dispatched to summon a hackney carriage to take him there.

Then, ignoring the disapproving looks from Lady Merriweather's staff, Ariel went upstairs. There she enlisted the help of Mrs. Merriweather's maid by the simple expedient of telling her it was to help ensure that lady's safety. The woman promised to slip out the back way, find a hackney, and have it waiting at the foot of the street at the appointed time. She would arrive at the museum ahead of Captain Stanfield and wait for him outside. Urgent message or no, Ariel had no intention of being so foolish as to enter the place at night all on her own. Not when two men had already been murdered there. No, she would wait for Captain Stanfield, for as long as it took, and then they would be in and out in under five minutes. If she was correct that whatever her father had hidden was indeed inside the second giraffe at the top of the stairs.

For a moment, Ariel had a qualm about having sent for Captain Stanfield to join her. She suspected that had her father thought of it, he would have included him in the people he said not to inform of what she was doing. But then, her father could not have guessed to what shifts she would be put to retrieve whatever it was he had hidden.

Once her arrangements were made with Mrs. Merriweather's maid, Ariel went to her own room to make other preparations before it was time to leave. Ariel sent the maid lent to her by Lady Merriweather to bed, telling her that she would undress herself when she was ready. The woman, annoyed to begin with that she had been assigned to such an unfashionable creature, made not the slightest argument, nor showed the slightest suspicion. Which was a fortunate circumstance, for she would undoubtedly have protested had she known what Ariel meant to do.

The moment she was gone, Ariel began to get ready. There was simply no excuse, she thought, as she tucked a dagger into one of the pockets under her dress, for a female to go haring off on some adventure without at least making an effort to prepare herself properly.

To be sure, there were those who would say she ought not to go to the museum. Not in the middle of the night at all, message or no message. But that would be very poor spirited of her. These same people would no doubt also disapprove of the dagger she carried, a present from her father so that he could be sure that she could defend herself in all the odd places they had visited over the years.

But Ariel believed in being prepared. It was the reason that every one of her gowns had pockets, even the newest ones from the fashionable mantua maker to whom Mrs. Merriweather had taken her. She had made the slits in the fabric herself and carefully stitched them so that no one would notice. A reticule was often far too much trouble, and this way the pockets she had tied on beneath her dress were always easy to hand. Now one carried the note from Stanfield and the dagger.

Into her other pocket, Ariel placed the unusually small pistol that her father had had made for her for just such a purpose as this. Not that her father had precisely anticipated his daughter meeting with a gentleman and slipping into the museum after hours when there might be killers about. But he had had it made for Ariel so that wherever she went, she would have a measure of protection for whatever circumstances in which she might find herself. How odd to think that England might turn out to be more dangerous than the other places for which both the pistol and the dagger had been intended!

At five minutes to the appointed time, Mrs. Merriweather's maid scratched on the door and then, as promised, showed her the back way out of the house, and soon she was in the carriage heading for the museum.

Marian had a horrible headache and it was growing worse by the moment. She wished only to return to Lady Merriweather's house. Perhaps she ought not to have had that last glass of champagne. She could not even recall who had offered some to Lady Merriweather and to her when they would have made good their escape a short time before.

But now she was determined. "Lady Merriweather, it really is growing late," she said. "Could we please leave?"

"Indeed, yes!" Lady Merriweather exclaimed. "I have the headache and wish for nothing more than to seek my bed. It was most foolish of you to insist that we come tonight. We are both of us too old for such nonsense."

There were amused glances at this exchange, but Marian was feeling far too cross to care. Instead, she accepted the offered assistance of a couple of the gentlemen to clear a path to the door for them, for there were still so many people in the ballroom that it was hard to move about.

Soon enough, though it felt as if it took forever, Lady and Mrs. Merriweather were handed in to Lady Merriweather's carriage and a rug tucked snugly over their laps. Neither lady took any note of the coachman, which was a mistake. Instead, the footman spoke briefly to the coachman, and soon the horses were moving quickly through the now deserted streets.

Marian could not have said what made her suddenly think something was wrong with the route the coachman was taking. She could not tell, in the darkness, after all, precisely by what streets they were going. Nor did she know which Lady Merriweather's coachman would normally have preferred. At first, she shrugged it all off as nothing with which they ought to concern themselves.

But Marian grew more and more uneasy as she realized that she was far more ill than should have been accounted for by the amount of champagne she had drunk during the evening. It was not the first time, after all, that she had been drugged, and when she realized the truth of the matter, she wondered why it had taken her as long as it did to recognize what was happening. And why she had not thought to take a closer look at the coachman before they climbed into the carriage.

Marian patted her pocket, grateful for the pistol there, and for the knife she had secreted on her person, for it looked as if she might very well need one or both of them. Her last thoughts, as she slipped into unconsciousness, was that the colonel would roast her unmercifully for this and that she was growing far too careless these days.

Neither lady was awake to notice when the carriage finally halted and strong hands lifted the pair of them out and into the museum.

Captain Stanfield sighed. The evening had proven even more tedious than usual and he could not say that he

had learned anything of use. How soon would Kinkaid
leave? he wondered.

At least Mrs. Merriweather and Lady Merriweather
were already gone. That was one less concern for William, for it had been an understood thing between him
and the colonel that he would keep an eye upon the
colonel's wife and see that she came to no harm. Still,
he wished their quarry would make a move. Not that he
was so certain, after tonight, that Kinkaid was the man
they were seeking.

William felt a twinge in his injured arm and frowned.
The last thing he needed was for his arm to truly become
incapacitated. The sling was supposed to serve as a dis-
guise, nothing more. And the old wound flared up rarely.
It was most annoying that it should choose this moment
to do so.

There! Kinkaid was moving toward the door. Stanfield
followed at a discreet distance, careful to speak to people
as he went so that his destination would not be so obvious. The trouble was that once you spoke to a lady, or
a gentleman, it was deucedly hard to get away.

For a moment, when he reached the door, Stanfield
feared that he had taken too long and that Kinkaid was
already on his way. But almost as though he had been
waiting for William, he stood across the street from the
Duchess of Berenford's town house, watching carriages
draw up to the door to take up their passengers and
deliver them safely home.

That circumstance gave Stanfield pause. His impulse, a
foolish one he knew, was to cross the street and confront
Kinkaid. But before he could decide precisely how to
proceed, a small boy ran up to William, asked if he was
Captain Stanfield, and when he said that he was, thrust
a piece of parchment into his hand, folded shut.

He unfolded it and realized it was from Miss Hawthorne asking him to meet her at the museum. The words
sent a cold chill through William. What the devil was she
doing going there at this time of night? Without a second
thought, he abandoned his intent to follow Kinkaid and

headed for the museum as quickly as he could. He hoped he was not too late, for the hour she mentioned was almost upon them. He wanted, he hoped, to arrive before Miss Hawthorne, and prevent her from ever entering that building. He never even noticed that Kinkaid began to follow *him*.

# 21

Lady Merriweather moaned. Marian wished she could kick her to be quiet, for in the darkness they had no way of knowing how close at hand their captors might be. They were somewhere in the museum; Marian was certain of it. And the fact that they were not bound and gagged, rather than cheering her, seemed to be a particularly bad sign. It meant, she thought, that whoever had brought them here had been certain they could find no means to escape.

Marian silently scolded herself for being so foolish as to be caught off guard in such a way. Even when she had surreptitiously disposed of the glass of champagne that Kinkaid had brought her, it was simply a precaution. She had all but decided he was not the villain, after all. Was she mistaken? Had he seen her dispose of the glass and arranged for another, or was she right that there was a different villain altogether?

Either way, she ought to have noticed that there was an odd taste to the champagne she drank later. Marian cudgeled her brains to recall who had handed that glass to her. The difficulty was that it had passed through many hands before finally being placed in her own. Nor could she recall who had first made the suggestion that they should all drink a toast, or even what the pretext had been.

Well, there was no point in wasting time. She had to get both herself and Lady Merriweather out of here before their captors returned. Marian tried to rise to her feet. That was when she realized that while her hands and mouth might have been left free, her ankles were tied to each other, and when she tried to move both feet together she found that they had also been tied to something immovable in the room. At the same moment, Marian discovered that someone had taken both her knife and her pistol from her.

Carefully, she reached down and tried to feel for what it was that circled her ankles and to what object it was attached. It was a rope, by the feel of it. Whatever it was tied to was out of her reach. Marian tugged at the rope, hoping that it might pull free, but it did not. Well, she thought, she would just have to try to untie the blasted thing!

Lady Merriweather apparently realized her situation at just that moment, for she began to complain in a loud, angry voice. "Where am I? Marian, are you here?"

"Yes, Lady Merriweather."

"Well, where are we and what are we doing here and why are we here? Who tied my ankles together? Untie them at once! I will not stand for such treatment!"

"I shall untie your ankles as soon as I have managed to untie mine," Marian replied calmly.

Apparently her calm infuriated Lady Merriweather, for she began to complain again. "Why aren't you shouting for help, then? We cannot stay here. We simply cannot! Are you not done yet? Oh, for heaven's sake, I suppose I must try to untie my ankles myself! This is your fault, you know."

"Mine?" Marian echoed, taken aback.

"It must be yours! No one could possibly wish *me* ill or think they had a right to kidnap me and tie me up! They must have been angry with you. I knew no good would come of my nephew marrying a former governess. I knew no good would come of his bringing you to London! I shan't forgive you, Marian, if anything happens to either of us."

Mrs. Merriweather wanted to say a great many things.

There were also a few things she might have liked to do to her husband's aunt, if she weren't a lady. Her main fear, however, was that Lady Merriweather's loud complaints would draw their kidnappers to them before she had managed to free her ankles and get them both out of there. She took in a breath to say so but didn't have the chance.

A large man, clad in dark clothing, suddenly stood before them. He held a lantern that cast very little light, and Marian thought that it looked remarkably like the sort that smugglers used. That is to say, there was a way to hide or shield the light until it was needed, without the lantern being extinguished completely. He wore a hood over his head, as did the men beside him. She wondered how long the villains had been standing there listening to them.

Lady Merriweather was no more pleased to see these fellows than Marian, but she seemed to think she could order them about as if they were her footmen.

"You, there! Untie our ankles at once!" Lady Merriweather commanded. "My cousin is a magistrate, and you will be very sorry if you don't!"

The man merely stood there. Lady Merriweather gasped in fury and began to ring a peal over his head. "This is an outrage, an outrage! How dare you treat me like this? I am a lady! We are both ladies! You have no right to treat us like this! Untie us at once! I will not tolerate such treatment. Do you realize that my gloves must be absolutely filthy? I doubt they shall ever come clean. I shall expect you to pay for another pair!"

Abruptly, the leader decided he had had enough. "If you want to live another fifteen minutes, my *lady*," he said in a voice that was dangerously quiet, "I suggest that you cease speaking at once!"

To Marian's astonishment, Lady Merriweather did so. But then, perhaps it was the shock of hearing a cultured voice, the voice of a gentleman, when Lady Merriweather must have been expecting an ordinary thief from the streets, that stopped her. A moment's reflection ought to have prepared her, but then Lady Merriweather was not given to reflection. And she was silent only for a moment.

"You are a gentleman," she said with great indignation.

He bowed. The hood he wore, however, muffled his voice as well as covered his face, so that neither Marian nor Lady Merriweather could possibly guess who he might be. "I am desolated to distress you," he said, with more than a trace of amusement in his voice, "but how did you think I managed to drug the both of you at the Duchess of Berenford's ball, if I were not in attendance as a gentleman?"

"You could have been a footman or other servant helping to serve the food and drink," Marian snapped, her own temper beginning to fray.

He bowed to her this time. "True." His voice was almost a caress as he added, "I knew you would see the possibilities better than she could. It is a very great pity that you chose to interfere with my . . . enterprise. I might otherwise have been able to admire your intelligence and determination to have what you desire."

"And what is that?" Marian asked, thinking to buy time and to discover more about their captor. After all, Colonel Merriweather must be here somewhere. If they were indeed in the museum, as she thought.

He laughed, a chillingly amiable laugh coming from a man who held them both captive. "Why, Mrs. Merriweather, obviously you desire respectability and acceptance among the *ton,* despite your years as a governess. And not one who was a shy and retiring creature either, I understand. One who was known as a tyrant in the households where she was employed. There are not many ladies who could manage such a feat. As I said, I admire your determination and ability to achieve what you desire. You married to advantage, and you carry off your new role with the same skill that you carried off the old one."

Marian held her breath. This man knew a great deal

about her, far too much for her comfort. Was this Kinkaid? He had, after all, known enough to call her Miss Tibbles at the ball. And yet, she did not think so. Whoever he was, it disturbed her that he knew so much. Even though he had said no more than anyone could easily have found out, it showed that someone had taken the trouble to ask. It showed that someone had known she would be his enemy. How much more did he know? She worried that it might very well be too much.

Beside her, Lady Merriweather once more took up her lament. "I told you it was your fault, Marian! I told you it was because of your unbecoming behavior and pursuits that we were in this ridiculous position! Now what do you have to say for yourself? And you, sir, you are behaving in the most ungentlemanly manner imaginable! What will your mother say when she learns you have behaved so disgracefully toward two helpless ladies? I expect you to release us and apologize at once!"

"Quiet!" the fellow snarled. He moved closer to Lady Merriweather, causing her to lean back in alarm. "You are alive only because of my admittedly grudging respect for Mrs. Merriweather. And because I believe she has information that could cause . . . difficulties for me—and because I believe that a note sent to her husband will bring him here straightway, as well. I have no interest or use for you. Unless, of course, you wish me to question you, instead? No? Then I should think twice about abusing her. You stay alive only so long as she does."

Lady Merriweather fell silent, thoroughly cowed, it seemed, by the fellow's unexpected anger. He turned again to Marian, and she felt a sinking sensation. So he meant to lure Andrew here? Because he thought they knew something? But what? What was it he thought they knew, and why was he so sure that they did? Was it Kinkaid? But even muffled as his voice was, Mrs. Merriweather did not think that was who stood before her. He was talking again, and she tried to focus on what he was saying, but it was difficult when her head ached so abominably!

"I am sorry to have to bring you here, Mrs. Merriweather. Even sorrier for what I shall have to do later. But such is life. I am glad, however, to have had the chance to tell you what worthy opponents I consider you and your husband to be. And now, if you will tell me what it is you and the colonel have discovered, I shall not need to cause more pain to either of you ladies than is absolutely necessary."

Marian groaned, as though her head ached even worse than it did. And as though she felt she might pass out at any moment. She let herself sway against Lady Merriweather, and she slurred her words as she replied. "I . . . No one . . . Andrew?"

The man gave a snort of disgust. "Very pretty acting, Mrs. Merriweather! A pity I don't believe you. But as you choose. I shall be back shortly to ask again. By then," he said to Lady Merriweather, "you had best hope she is ready to answer me, or perhaps I shall begin with you, after all."

He bowed a final time and then retreated with the others into the darkness, his lantern once more shielded. Marian felt both relief and dismay. He was giving them a short reprieve, no doubt to increase their fear of what he might do, but they could not count on it lasting long. They had to get free, and do so as quickly as possible!

Marian had to fight a sense of growing panic as she tried futilely to undo the rope at her ankles. She was close to an unaccustomed bout of tears when abruptly Lady Merriweather's voice came from beside her, low and calm.

"Here, my dear. Would you like a knife?"


The streets near the museum were deserted. There was no moon tonight, and Ariel found herself grateful for the darkness. The coachman had followed her orders and halted some two or three streets away from her true destination. She opened the door of the hackney and looked up and down the street. Had there been anyone about, she might have risked asking the coachman to drive her straight to the door, gauging the danger from men on the street to be greater than that of being so visible arriving there.

But since the streets were deserted, she decided to risk going the final distance on foot. She paid the driver and began to step out.

He hesitated. "I mislike this, miss," he said. "I mislike setting you 'ere when there's no one about."

"I shall be fine," she promised. "But I should like you to wait here until I return. I shall be generous, if you will. Here is half now, and there is just as much again if you are waiting when I return."

The man hesitated a moment more, then nodded. Not for the likes of him to judge the madness of his betters! Still, he didn't like it. Didn't like it one bit. He couldn't help worrying what he would do if his daughter ever took such a dangerous start.

But Ariel was already in the shadows, and when he looked one last time to see how she was, he thought she must have vanished into the nearest building and he felt a sense of relief. Perhaps she would be all right, after all.

Ariel continued to hug the shadows as she made her way to the museum. She did so instinctively, not knowing that it was what Stanfield or the colonel would have recommended had she been able to ask them. She also held in one hand the keys to the museum, so that she could enter quickly once Captain Stanfield arrived, and so that they would not jangle in her pocket or her reticule. Her other hand was securely clamped around the dagger in her pocket. She was not, she vowed, going to find herself in the helpless position so many foolish young ladies did in the novels in Lady Merriweather's library!

No one, however, tried to stop her. The streets continued to appear deserted, or so it seemed, until she had almost reached her goal. Then a carriage came rattling down the street and halted not very far away from her.

Ariel moved even farther into the shadows. She could see men leaving the entrance to the museum, hoods over their heads, and moments later, two still bodies being carried from the carriage and through the door into the museum grounds. Where was the porter? she wondered. She moved closer and tried to set aside her shock and see more clearly who was being carried into the museum. It appeared to be two women, and Ariel could not help fearing that one must be Mrs. Merriweather. The other might very well have been the colonel's aunt. It was not a pleasant thought. Particularly since neither woman stirred as she was carried inside.

It would have done no good to show herself, Ariel knew. The dagger in her pocket was unlikely to frighten these men. And even if she shot one with her pistol, the others would have no trouble capturing her afterward, in spite of the dagger. So she simply watched, hoping she would find a way to help.

After a few moments, the carriage set off down the street and around the corner, where it drew to a halt all but out of sight. Well, that reduced by one, at any rate, the number of men to be reckoned with. The rest of the men disappeared into the museum.

Ariel waited a moment, then slipped across the street. The porter was sound asleep, slumped against the doorway. When she could not wake him, Ariel hesitated. She ought to wait for Captain Stanfield, but if she did so, who knew what would happen to the two women? In the end, she went through the door after the others, but not before she dropped a lacy handkerchief where it gleamed brightly against the dark ground. If the men saw it, they would no doubt think it had fallen from one of the unconscious women. But Captain Stanfield, she hoped, would realize it meant she had been here and gone inside.

In spite of her hesitation, Ariel was in time to see the

men and the two unconscious women enter a side door, rather than the main entrance of the museum. She followed, keeping to the shadows as much as she could, and found they had left the side door unlocked. That was convenient but implied that perhaps someone meant to use it again soon and she had best get out of sight as quickly as possible.

There were advantages to having spent so much time in the museum, both as a woman and a child. Ariel knew all the hiding places and all the different ways to get from one point to another, even in the dark. That gave her a great advantage over the others. The difficulty was to know what she should do first. Should she try to find the colonel or the Bow Street Runner and let them know what she had seen? Or should she try to find the women who had been carried in first?

The sensible answer was easy. She should find the two men. She should warn them about what she had seen and have their assistance in trying to rescue the women. The only difficulty with that was that she had no idea where they were inside the museum. How was she to find them without knowing or risking running into the others? They would, after all, be as careful as she was to keep to the shadows and make themselves hard to be seen. Nor could she blunder about, trying to get their attention, for the result would almost certainly be that she would end up in the wrong hands. It was a dilemma and one she needed to sort out quickly.

Ariel might or might not have been reassured to know that Captain Stanfield entered the museum not long after she did. He came in, however, by way of the front door. He had indeed found the handkerchief and correctly interpreted what it meant. He had also noted, with a frown, that the porter seemed sound asleep on the job. He could not rouse the fellow and he wasted very little time trying to do so. Instead, he hurried his steps toward the main entrance of the museum.

Once inside, he moved with the same stealth as Ariel, the same caution for the risk of being seen or heard. He moved more slowly, however, for he was not as familiar with the museum as she was. And he moved without any notion what his destination might be.

In the darkness, Colonel Merriweather felt a twinge of unease. Something felt very wrong here tonight. And yet, he had not heard or seen anything out of place. He was keeping guard over the main door. Collins, meanwhile, was upstairs at a window overlooking the courtyard, watching in case anyone should try to enter by another door.

Collins and Merriweather were supposed to have the place to themselves. Aside from the porter outside, no one else should be here, for Tom had not yet been replaced as night watchman. But the colonel reminded himself that no one had tried to enter tonight, at least not since he had come on guard. And if the Runner had seen anyone, surely he would have raised the alarm.

Still, the colonel felt that same twinge of unease again. Almost, he worried about Marian. But that was absurd! She was safely at the Duchess of Berenford's ball, and after that she would go straight home. She had promised him that she would. So why the devil was he thinking of her just now? If he were to worry about anyone, he ought to worry about Captain Stanfield. Had the young man been able to follow Kinkaid? Were they on their way to the museum? If so, when were they most likely to arrive?

There was a motion at the front door, and the colonel drew his pistol just in case. He leaned back farther into the shadows and waited. Whoever it was, was about to suffer a severe shock, he thought with grim satisfaction.

Instead, it was the colonel who suffered the shock when he realized that the person entering the museum was Captain Stanfield, and that he was alone. He watched, thinking that perhaps the younger man was luring someone here, or that he was someone's prisoner. But no one else came in, and after a moment the colonel frowned. Had he misjudged the younger man? Did he have plans of his own? The only way to find out, he decided, was to follow Stanfield deeper into the museum.

With a sigh of disgust, he did so.

# 22

Marian gratefully accepted the knife from Lady Merriweather and quickly used it to cut the rope from her ankles. She did not bother to ask where it came from. There would be time enough to discover that later, assuming they managed to leave safely. Once her ankles were free, she gave the knife back to Lady Merriweather who tucked it away under her skirts again.

Then with a touch on the arm, Lady Merriweather indicated that she wished to be going. Marian was not about to disagree. Together they silently rose to their feet and lifted their skirts so that they could move more quietly. Given that they had no notion where they were in the museum, it was not an easy thing to find their way without bumping into things. But neither woman wanted to remain where she was.

Unfortunately, they had not even reached the doorway when a lantern flashed in front of them once again. It was useless to try to hide, useless to pretend they were still tied at the ankles.

"Well, well," the gentleman they had seen before said with what might almost have been approval in his voice. "You are more resourceful than I anticipated, Mrs. Merriweather. I shall be very sorry to have to kill you out of hand. But I will if you give me any more trouble. Or perhaps I will kill her, instead."

This last was said in a menacing growl, and both women fell back when faced with his anger and the pistol in his hand. Over his shoulder, the gentleman snarled at someone to tie them up again.

"And this time tie their wrists behind them as well," he ordered. Then, indicating Mrs. Merriweather, he added, "Search this one again. Look for a knife or other weapon. I do not trust her!"

In that moment, Marian was very glad she had given the knife back to Lady Merriweather. She only hoped the colonel's aunt would find a chance to use it to good advantage. Not that she meant to let them tie her up at all, if she could help it. If the chance came, she would crash into the man reaching for her and try to dash past the gentleman with the lantern. Particularly if she could find a means to put the lantern out as she did so.

Lady Merriweather, it seemed, had precisely the same thought, for out of the corner of her eye, Marian saw her put out a foot and neatly trip the man reaching for *her*. Marian promptly grabbed the nearest object and thrust it against her captor's chest. Instinctively, he reached to grab it, and she darted past. Startled, the man with the lantern had no time to aim his pistol before Marian and Lady Merriweather both crashed into him, each from one side, sending his lantern to the floor where it went out.

And then they were past the villains. Both ladies moved as quickly as they could, all too aware of the shouts of outrage behind them. If they were caught, it would not be pleasant. But then, if they didn't escape, if they didn't run now, things would be just as unpleasant anyway. A moment later, as they passed a doorway, a small hand reached out and grabbed Marian's sleeve. She would have struck at the person save that a whispered voice said, "It is I, Miss Hawthorne. Come this way, quickly!"

So instead of striking the person who grasped her arm, Marian reached out and grabbed Lady Merriweather's. "This way," she whispered, not stopping to argue.

They could have had no better guide, Marian thought, than Miss Hawthorne, to help them slip away from the

men pursuing them. She was very glad to see that Lady
Merriweather was quick-witted enough to agree and
come without protest. It made her begin to wonder just
how much had been the true Lady Merriweather and
how much had been performance when the colonel's
aunt had been berating their captors.

Almost against her will, Marian found her estimation
of the other lady rising rapidly. When all of this was
over and resolved successfully, she hoped, she was
going to have a great many questions to put to Lady
Merriweather!

Captain Stanfield was growing more and more uneasy.
He had seen no sign of Miss Hawthorne other than the
handkerchief outside, and he was beginning to wonder if
he was on a fool's errand. And yet he could not simply
leave, not when she might be in trouble or need him
here.

Suddenly he heard shouts deep in the museum. The
voices were those of men, not a woman, but William ran
in that direction anyway. Either he would be in time to
help capture the thieves or to rescue Miss Hawthorne.
Though if those shouts were her doing, then she had
perhaps taken care of that little matter herself.

Still, he did move with some caution, for it had occurred to him to wonder if the note really had been from
Miss Hawthorne. Or whether it had been meant to lure
him here to be captured. In that event, even the shouts
ahead might be part of the plan. So he moved swiftly,
but with caution.

Suddenly he heard a muffled sound behind him, as if
someone had tripped, and he heard a soft cry of dismay.
William turned and crouched, ready to fend off an attack.
A moment later he realized that the person following
him, who had fallen over some object, was Colonel Merriweather. Stanfield went and offered a hand to help
him up.

The colonel muttered a soft curse and said, "What the devil are you doing here? You were supposed to be following Kinkaid!"

"I was handed a note from Miss Hawthorne asking me to meet her outside the museum," Stanfield explained. "I could not take the chance she would be foolish enough to come inside alone if I failed her, and it seems, since I was late, she did, for I found her handkerchief on the ground in the doorway."

The colonel cursed a trifle more fluently this time, but still softly. "Do you think she could be the cause of the shouts we heard?"

"That is my fear," Stanfield agreed.

"Then we had best find out."

The colonel took the lead and William allowed him to do so. The older man, after all, had spent more nights here in the museum than Stanfield and might know better how to proceed. Still, they moved with a caution that could not help but cause William to worry that they would not reach Miss Hawthorne in time—if they found her at all.

What if the noises ahead simply ceased? How would they find where anyone was? And then, just as Stanfield had that thought, the sounds did cease. He and the colonel immediately halted. "What now?" he whispered to Merriweather.

The colonel took a long time to answer. "I wish to heaven I knew! I also wish I knew what happened to our Bow Street Runner. Collins ought to have come and gotten me the moment they entered the museum. He was to be watching from an upstairs window in case they came in by another entrance. We'd best try to find him first. We could use another ally. Especially since it sounds to me like there are several scoundrels moving about the place."

Stanfield nodded. He didn't like the delay, but he could not argue with the common sense behind the plan. He only hoped that if Miss Hawthorne was here and a prisoner, she had somehow managed to slip free of her captors. Or, if not, that her captors did not yet mean to harm her.

In fact, it was Ariel, Mrs. Merriweather, and Lady Merriweather who found Collins first. They weren't trying to do so. Indeed, they had no notion where he might be hiding. They were simply attempting to stay out of sight and reach of the villains pursuing them.

But when they slipped into a room that Ariel knew would take them to another part of the museum, she tripped over something that ought not to have been in the middle of the floor. It was, they all realized very quickly, the Bow Street Runner.

"Is he dead?" Ariel whispered to Mrs. Merriweather, who was feeling the man's face.

"No, just stunned, I think. He seems to have a blow to the back of his head."

"Here, use this under his nose. It might bring him around, if anything can," Lady Merriweather whispered, holding out a tiny vinaigrette she must have been carrying in the reticule that hung from her wrist.

The smelling salts did indeed revive the injured Runner. He started to moan. Mrs. Merriweather promptly clapped a hand over his mouth. That caused him to begin to thrash about in earnest, and Ariel feared he would injure himself even further. Or worse, injure one of them by mistake.

"Quiet, Mr. Collins," she hissed at him. "There are men here who mean to kill all of us, and you will bring them down upon our heads if you are not quiet!"

At the sound of her voice, the Runner instantly went very still. Mrs. Merriweather risked removing her hand and helped him to a sitting position. He looked at them in the darkness and shook his head.

"This oughtn't to be 'appening," he said in a whisper. "The colonel will 'ave me 'ead if 'e finds you 'ere."

"In that case," Lady Merriweather whispered in a

practical voice, "we had better get out of here so that he doesn't, hadn't we?"

The Runner started to nod, then stopped, obviously realizing it was not a motion his injured head would appreciate. Instead, he rose to his feet, leaning on both Ariel and Mrs. Merriweather for support.

The Runner was shrewd enough, however, to say to Ariel, "You lead the way, missy. You knows this place better'n the rest of us."

"Hold hands. It will be too dark to see through much of the way," Ariel warned.

When they were all in a line, holding hands, she began to lead them through the warren of rooms. She moved slowly, cautiously, for as well as she knew the place, Ariel could not remember the placement of every object, and she did not wish to risk any of them knocking over anything. She also kept to the walls as much as she could.

The Runner seemed to approve, for at one point he whispered, "Very wise, missy. If they does come inter the same room along of us, their lanterns won't cast light to where we be 'iding. Very wise, indeed."

Unfortunately, they needed luck as much as they needed wisdom. Ariel hoped that by leading her group toward a door other than the one by which they had all entered, she would evade the thieves and kidnappers. They would, presumably, expect the ladies to head for the nearest means of escape.

At one point she thought she heard a noise nearby. It could not have been her imagination because all of them froze into place at precisely the same moment, clearly alarmed by the same sound. Someone was moving about nearby. Ariel held her breath. Had they guessed what she meant to do? Or was it Captain Stanfield? Had he seen the handkerchief and followed her into the museum after all?

Ariel did not dare take the risk of finding out. First she must help to get Mrs. Merriweather and the colonel's aunt safely out of the museum. Only then could she think what to do about her appointment with Captain Stanfield and whatever it was that her father had left inside the stuffed giraffe.

So she stayed very still and waited. Only when it was clear that the sounds were moving away from them did she take another step, still leading her group toward a way out. They might well have made it, too, if she hadn't tripped. And if Lady Merriweather's skirts hadn't gotten caught on some object and pulled it from its display. The object crashed down onto the floor.

They froze, the whole group, listening. Had they been heard? Were the villains close enough to the sound to follow it straight to them? Ariel hesitated, uncertain what to do next. She could hear something, but the sounds seemed to be coming both from behind and ahead of them. Without a word, she quickly drew her group to stand flat against the wall, and they all held their breath as someone, or perhaps more than one person, passed through the very room they were in. In the complete darkness, they could neither see nor be seen. Only when she was sure that whoever it was had not spotted them, did Ariel begin to move again.

Captain Stanfield heard a crash in one of the rooms ahead of them. He and the colonel moved quickly but cautiously in that direction.

There was more noise, voices now, and a distant gleam of light. William paused and felt the colonel stop beside him as well.

"Shall we stay put and let them come to us?" Stanfield suggested.

Even in the dark, William could tell the colonel smiled. "You'd have made a good commanding officer," Merriweather whispered approvingly. "We shall indeed stay put. Except that I should like you to take up position against one wall and I shall take up position over by the other wall. We shall hold this rope taut between us."

William didn't argue. He grabbed the end of the rope the colonel held out to him. There was, he knew, no time to waste upon foolish questions, such as how the colonel came to have a rope with him. William moved swiftly and silently across the hall, and in moments they had the rope taut between them at the height of a man's knees.

They were just in time. Scarcely were both men, and the rope, in place, than several dark figures came rushing down the hallway and straight into the trap William and the colonel had set for them. Just as planned, the men went tumbling onto their faces, and before they could recover, both Stanfield and Merriweather had pistols aimed at the head of the man he judged to be their leader.

"Tell your men to yield," Colonel Merriweather said loudly, "or I shall shoot you!"

Unfortunately, the others appeared not to care what happened to their leader. One grabbed Merriweather about the ankles and pulled him to the ground. Another man reached for William, intending to do the same to him, but he managed to move just out of reach. And then they heard the voices both men least wished to hear.

"Andrew?"

"William? Captain Stanfield?"

The Bow Street Runner's voice, on the other hand, was very welcome, indeed. " 'ere now! Let 'im up! I've got me popper, oi do!"

"No, you don't," the gentleman objected. "My men took it from you when they bashed you over the head."

His words were enough to shake the spell, and before anyone knew what was happening, the scoundrels were on their feet and holding Miss Hawthorne and Mrs. Merriweather with knives to their throats. Lady Merriweather they ignored as insignificant. All she could do, it seemed, was stand and wail bitterly at their situation.

As the colonel gave a cry of dismay and struggled to reach his wife, the gentleman stepped forward and pointed his pistol, first at the colonel and then at Stanfield.

"Do not go any closer to them!" the villain warned both men. Then, in a quieter voice he added, "I think, gentlemen, that the tide has turned. You are, it would seem, in my power. If you would all be so good as to place your pistols upon the floor . . ."

When they had done so, the villain came closer.

"What are you going to do to us?" Colonel Merriweather demanded.

"You are getting far too impertinent in your inquiries, all of you. In a few moments, you will all be dead, the unfortunate victims of a last massive theft here at the museum, and I and my friends will be long gone."

"Lord Hollis?" Ariel gasped.

The villain's pistol wavered, but only for a moment. "You are mistaken, Miss Hawthorne! Perhaps you ought to have worn your spectacles."

"No, you *are* Lord Hollis," she said with quiet conviction. "I would recognize your voice anywhere."

"But I thought you suspected Mr. Kinkaid," Lady Merriweather protested.

Hollis gaped at her. "Kinkaid? But I thought—" He broke off abruptly. "Apparently I miscalculated how much all of you knew. But no matter. You are here, and I have no choice but to kill all of you."

What happened next, all of them would remember to their dying days with a sense of utter disbelief. Lady Merriweather tottered toward their captor.

"Please let us go!" she cried.

As everyone turned toward her, she grasped for his sleeve and he laughed harshly in her face. Then, so swiftly that none of them understood for a moment what they were seeing, a knife flashed in Lady Merriweather's hand and she stabbed the villain in the throat.

At the same time, Mrs. Merriweather rammed her elbow into the stomach of the man behind her and twisted free. By her side, Miss Hawthorne was scarcely a moment behind. She did something that caused the man holding her to let go as well.

The two men tried to grab their captives again, but each of the ladies found an object to smash against the villains' faces. From there it was a simple matter for the

Runner to grab one man, and the colonel and Stanfield to retrieve their pistols and point them at the other men.

"That will be quite enough!" Colonel Merriweather said, finding his voice at last.

"Quite enough," his aunt echoed with understandable satisfaction.

William looked at the Runner. "What now, Mr. Collins?" he asked.

It was Ariel who answered. "There is a carriage, out front, down the street and around the corner from the museum. There was one driver and no one else that I saw. And I asked the hackney driver who brought me to wait; he is a couple of streets away in the other direction. We could bundle them into those two carriages and take them to Bow Street, couldn't we?"

"We would not all fit," Mrs. Merriweather said briskly, "but that is irrelevant. I should be quite happy to allow the colonel and Captain Stanfield and our Runner to take them along. If, that is, they believe they can manage. That was quite a severe blow to your head," she told the Runner.

"We'll manage," he growled.

"Yes, of course we can manage," the colonel said impatiently. "Particularly after you tie them up with the rope you'll find on the floor. That's what I brought it here for. Tie them all up, even Lord Hollis and this fellow. I don't care how injured we may think them to be, I don't wish to take chances that we are mistaken."

It was as they reached for the rope that everything happened at once. The villain, who had been stabbed, suddenly dove for the floor, oblivious to his injury. He rolled once and came back to his feet, the colonel's forgotten pistol in hand.

Before anyone seemed to have time to react, a shot rang out and the villain sank to the floor. As he fell, he said in disbelief, "Miss Hawthorne?"

It was then that they all realized it was Ariel who had pulled out a pistol and shot the fellow. She walked closer to him. In a gentle voice, she said, "Unfortunately for you, Lord Hollis, I never truly did need those spectacles. I can see quite well without them."

Several voices murmured astonishment. Ariel ignored all of them. Instead she turned to the others and said, "You mentioned some rope?"

There was plenty of rope, fortunately, and Stanfield, Merriweather, and Ariel all produced knives with which to cut it. They could even have used Lady Merriweather's knife—if they didn't mind a little blood—but it was not, fortunately, necessary.

Once all the men were safely tied up, William looked at the ladies. "We shall get the men to Bow Street, but what are we to do about the three of you?"

It was Lady Merriweather who answered. "We shall wait here at the museum, of course," she said briskly. "After you've taken these villains to Bow Street, you can come back with the carriages and take us home."

"I don't like it, Marian," Colonel Merriweather said bluntly.

"Neither do I," Mrs. Merriweather retorted, "but I can see no other solution."

Reluctantly it was settled. Pistols were reloaded and left with the ladies, just in case there should be any villains that had not been caught. They elected to wait in what had once been Hawthorne's office. Over the most vocal protests of Mrs. Merriweather, Ariel left long enough to go to the stuffed giraffe at the head of the main staircase.

There she found a thick sheaf of papers, and by the light of one of the villains' lanterns she looked them over. It was enough to explain everything, and it was with a constriction to her throat that she tucked them inside her bodice and rejoined the other two ladies in her father's old office. Somehow it did not surprise her that when the men returned, Mr. Kinkaid was with them.

# 23

Mrs. Merriweather, Colonel Merriweather, Miss Hawthorne, Captain Stanfield, Mr. Kinkaid, and Lady Merriweather all stared at one another in the gathering light of early morning in her ladyship's drawing room. Every one of them held a glass of brandy.

Servants were beginning to stir below stairs and noises could be heard in the street as other households came to life as well. A maid entered the room to clean the grate, then backed out hastily when she realized that the room was not empty, as she had expected it to be.

"I fear we have shocked your staff," Stanfield told Lady Merriweather.

"Do them good!" she retorted, draining her glass of brandy.

She held the empty glass out to her nephew, who took it with good humor and refilled it for her. "Tell me, Aunt Cordelia, how you came to have a knife upon you tonight," Colonel Merriweather said as he did so. "Mind you, I am very glad that you did. I just would like to know why on earth you should have carried a knife to a ball."

Lady Merriweather cast a reproving look upon him. "I read," she said.

"Novels!" the colonel could not help but reply, a hint of contempt in his voice.

She shrugged. "As you say, novels. And I know them to be foolish nonsense. But they also give one pause.

Bad things do happen to ladies—even here in London. I know more than one lady assaulted in the past year. Why should I not carry a means to defend myself? Particularly when all of you cannot seem to keep from getting involved in the most ridiculously dangerous circumstances?"

"But to a ball?" Mrs. Merriweather protested.

Lady Merriweather lifted an eyebrow. "Well? Was I mistaken in doing so?" She paused and then added, "Perhaps you had not heard, but one of the ladies I spoke of was accosted returning home from a ball. Footpads stopped her carriage. Had she had a knife with which to defend herself, she need never have lost the diamond necklace that she prized so highly."

The colonel grinned. "You are a right one, Aunt Cordelia," he said.

Lady Merriweather sniffed, but there was no hiding her delight at the compliment. She did, however, turn a stern gaze upon Captain Stanfield, who had discarded his sling and cane and held his glass of brandy in the hand that was supposed to have been all but useless.

"What about you?" Lady Merriweather demanded of the young man. "Why were you pretending to be injured far more severely than you obviously are?"

"So that anyone seeing me would underestimate my ability to defend myself, of course," he answered promptly. "Just as no one would expect an elegant lady such as yourself to carry or wield a knife, no one would expect me to be able to disarm a man or knock him to the ground or carry a pistol hidden inside the sling."

She nodded grudgingly, then turned to Mrs. Merriweather. "You are the one I find a sad disappointment, Marian. Why were you not carrying a knife?"

"I was," Marian replied with a grim edge to her voice. "I had a knife and a pistol on my person. Both of which the villains apparently expected me to have, because they searched me and found both and removed them before I regained my wits at the museum."

"Oh. Very well. I forgive you, then," Lady Merriweather said magnanimously. She turned to Ariel. "And you, Miss Hawthorne! Let this be a warning to you to always go about with some means to defend yourself!"

"Oh, I had such means," Ariel replied coolly. She pulled her small pistol out of her pocket. "This is what I used to shoot Lord Hollis. Papa commissioned this for me years ago. I didn't show it at the museum, for I didn't think it would frighten the men we were dealing with. They might not believe I could really kill a man with it, and I would get only one shot."

She allowed the others to hand it around and remark over the cleverness of the design. Then she pulled the knife from her other pocket and showed that as well. "I also used this to stab into the leg of the man who was holding me," Ariel said. "But I had to wait, you see, until there was at least some chance of success. I did not wish to risk doing so until I was certain Mrs. Merriweather would also manage to break free of her captor."

"What about you, Mr. Kinkaid?" Lady Merriweather demanded. "What were you doing outside the museum? And since you were there, why didn't you come in to help?"

Mr. Kinkaid bowed. "I followed Captain Stanfield. I thought it might prove interesting, and I was quite correct. Had I known just how interesting things were inside the museum, I promise I would have come in to help. But I had no notion. Still, I do think I acquitted myself rather well when I assisted Captain Stanfield in removing the villains' coachman from his perch."

Captain Stanfield grinned. He couldn't help himself.

"What," Lady Merriweather asked in the frostiest of voices, "is so amusing, young man?"

He looked around the room, then back at her. "I was thinking that none of us were as we seemed. Except, perhaps, Colonel Merriweather. The rest of us were all far more formidable than anyone could have guessed. Can you imagine how disconcerting it must have been for the men we captured?"

"One might almost feel sorry for them," Lady Merriweather said tartly, "if they weren't such fools. Tell me, Andrew. Who were the others? Besides Lord Hollis?"

"Simple cutthroats and ruffians," Colonel Merriweather replied. "Except for one we discovered to be a clerk at the museum. It seems he believed himself to be woefully underpaid. Fellow comes of a good family, but he is the younger son of a younger son. Apparently he felt humiliated that he was forced to work after his efforts to marry an heiress failed. So he began to help Hollis steal artifacts from the museum. I am certain you must know him, Miss Hawthorne. His name is Henry Gilmer."

"Yes, I do," Ariel acknowledged. She paused and took a deep breath. Then she went on. "I know far more than that. My father found out about Mr. Gilmer and left an account for me hidden at the museum. I've barely had time to skim over what he wrote, but, well, it begins, I think, with Mr. Kinkaid." She turned to him. "Perhaps you would care to explain?"

Kinkaid sighed, then cleared his throat. "Yes, perhaps I'd better," he agreed. He looked at the others. "Hawthorne wanted funds to travel, the way he used to do before he ran through his own inheritance. In particular, he wanted to go to Egypt to see what he could find to bring back to the museum. We talked about it, Hawthorne and I, and we agreed he would lend me some artifacts from the museum in exchange for a good-size payment. He didn't ask for enough to travel, just enough to invest. He figured that if those investments were successful, he'd be able to pay me back, I would return the artifacts from the museum, and he would get to go on his trip. I was never to keep them permanently. I suppose we shouldn't have done it, either of us, but it seemed like a way for both of us to have what we wanted, and no one hurt by it."

There was a stunned silence. It was Ariel who broke it. "That was the start of the trouble. At some point, Mr. Gilmer began to steal artifacts from the museum and sell them to Lord Hollis. When Papa realized what was going on, he did not know how to stop them without exposing his own actions as well. He meant well, when he entered into this scheme with Mr. Kinkaid. But he knew how it would look to others."

She paused and looked across the room. "My father sent for you, Colonel Merriweather, to help. But when he saw you, he lost his courage. He feared that perhaps Mr. Gilmer had gotten the notion to steal from discovering what he had done. Papa could not bear what you would think of him, if you knew."

"So he decided to try to stop Gilmer on his own?" Stanfield said, when Ariel's voice faltered. "Perhaps he hoped to redeem himself by doing so, even at the risk of his own safety?"

Ariel nodded, grateful for his understanding. "Papa knew the odds were against him, and he wrote this all out and hid it at the museum, then arranged that if anything should happen to him, a letter would be delivered to me telling me where to find these pages. He thought ten days would be sufficient to throw off the scent for anyone who might suspect me of knowing what was going on. He didn't, you see, wish to put me at risk. The rest, well, Papa meant to confront Lord Hollis and Mr. Gilmer together, and I can only guess that when he did so, they killed him."

She broke off then, her face very pale. Stanfield reached out to Ariel and drew her to him. She buried her face against his chest.

Again there was silence. Then Mrs. Merriweather said slowly, "And it seems Mr. Gilmer or Lord Hollis did suspect that Hawthorne might have written something down, because they sent someone to Miss Hawthorne's house the day her father died, presumably to find out."

"I think it most likely," the colonel agreed. "I would guess they also decided to hurry along their plans to take what they could from the museum—just in case. Tom must have come upon the men the next night, and they killed him."

"But why had he not happened upon them before?" Lady Merriweather asked.

"Perhaps Mr. Hawthorne had always told him to stay in his room at night," Stanfield suggested. "Or perhaps Gilmer usually gave him a sleeping draught on nights things were to be taken out of the museum, and that particular night he forgot or Tom was too upset to drink it. In any event, on that particular night, Tom interrupted the thieves and they killed him."

Mrs. Merriweather regarded Ariel with what seemed to her to be a worried eye. And when the former governess spoke, worry seemed to be in her voice as well. "How much of this will become public?" she asked her husband.

The colonel gave a cynical, wry smile. "Not a great deal, I'll wager. In the end, I would guess Lord Hollis will return the artifacts to the museum and the museum will decline to press charges, with the understanding that Hollis leave the country at once. Mr. Gilmer's family may also choose to pay some sort of restitution to the museum and arrange that he is never again seen in England. The other footpads and the coachmen will in all likelihood be transported. As for Mr. Kinkaid, here, well, I presume there is no law against being loaned artifacts with the consent of the curator. Particularly if they are returned immediately."

Kinkaid bowed. "Of course. They shall be returned by the end of the day."

Ariel turned to face him, Stanfield's arm still around her waist. "If you will tell me how much my father owed you, I shall arrange for my father's solicitor to return the funds at once."

Kinkaid shook his head. "No. On the whole, I think I should prefer that you keep the money, Miss Hawthorne. Under the circumstances, I think I should rather not have it back. Rest assured I can well afford to refuse to accept it."

"Never mind that," Lady Merriweather said sharply. "What I want to know is what you mean to do, Miss Hawthorne? You are not, I trust, going to go into a decline? You're not such a missish creature as that!"

Ariel drew a breath to answer, but Captain Stanfield forestalled her. "Miss Hawthorne and I need to talk before she can answer your question," he said. "I presume I may use one of your other rooms to speak with her?"

He did not wait for an answer, but took Ariel by the hand and pulled her out of the room before anyone could have time to object. Down the hall they went and into the room at the end, without the slightest hesitation. But once there, his manner became markedly diffident.

"Miss Hawthorne, I know that it is very soon after your father's death. And perhaps you will think me impertinent anyway. But, Miss Hawthorne, will you do me the honor of becoming my wife?"

Ariel stared at him. "Truly? Even after what you have learned tonight about my father?"

"Even after tonight," he agreed. Then, teasingly, he added, "I must marry you, you know. Think of my mother and sisters! They would never forgive me if I don't!"

Ariel stiffened. She meant to draw away. Or at least remove her hand from his grasp. But he wouldn't let her. Instead, before she could object to his teasing words, he kissed her on the forehead and said, "And I must marry you because in no other way will I find peace. In no other way will I find someone to make my life complete. I love you, Ariel."

"And I love you . . . William."

"So you will marry me?"

She started to say "yes," but suddenly all the old fears and suspicions rushed back. Ariel pulled her hand free, and she stepped back several paces.

"I am not so sure," she said. "What will you expect me to do?"

"Do?" Stanfield echoed, clearly taken aback.

"Yes. Do," Ariel repeated, almost fiercely. "I am a scholar, not a . . . a lady trained to pour tea and hold parties and . . . and such."

He grinned. "I don't want you to pour tea or hold parties and such," he promptly said.

That only angered Ariel more. "You are roasting me, but this is not a jesting matter. I am *not* a lady, whatever my provenance might be! I am a scholar, and I must know whether you will respect that or not, before I can know whether it would be wise for me to marry you."

"Wise?"

Stanfield quirked an eyebrow upward as he said the word, and the corners of his lips twitched as though he were trying not to smile. He moved toward Ariel, forcing her to back away, until she found herself pressed against the far wall.

"I don't know if it would be wise," William said amiably, "for you to marry me. Indeed, I think it probably would not be. But I hope it will be an adventure, for both of us."

"Adventure?" It was Ariel's turn to echo a word.

William nodded and moved even closer, so that he could put his hands on her shoulders. "I do not want a milk-and-water miss. I should be bored to tears by a lady who conceived her whole purpose to be as an ornament and to preside over parties and tea trays. I find that I want a wife with a mind to match my own. One with sufficient courage not to shirk from adventures, either."

He paused and smiled that sweet smile that had tumbled Ariel's heart about so many times already.

"Marry me," he said, his voice soft and coaxing. "We shall travel—wherever you wish to go. You shall show me the places you have been and I shall take you to the places you've always wanted to go. I cannot swear that I shall make you happy, but I think I can promise you that we shall never be bored. Please, Ariel? Will you marry me?"

"Yes," she said softly. "With all my heart, I will."

# Epilogue

Ariel glanced up at the man beside her. William stood tall, no cane or sling in sight. He had been a source of strength for her, since her father died. More than that, his voice, his touch, his very gaze upon her face stirred up feelings inside that she had never known before. And today they were to be married. Stanfield's family had rallied around her, and their kindness, as well as that of Lady Merriweather, had done much to smooth her path among the *ton*.

Now they were saying their vows. Ariel was very much aware of the colonel and Mrs. Merriweather behind her. It was a source of amusement to everyone that the former governess was increasing. Lady Merriweather had even been heard to remark upon the possibility of twins. Children. Would she and William have children? Ariel wondered. Perhaps they would have a daughter as full of life and mischief as Mrs. Merriweather's Elizabeth. Or a son, one who looked just like William. The thought made her smile.

But Ariel's thoughts of the Merriweathers were also inextricably tied with thoughts of her father. How she wished he were here to see her today!

Some shadow of unhappiness must have crossed Ariel's face, for William squeezed her hand reassuringly, and she smiled up at him. Here was her refuge, her shelter. How strange it felt to be taken care of by someone else! And yet, it was wonderful, as well.

Beside her, Stanfield smiled, too. He had not thought to find love or a desire to wed. For so long he had resisted the lures thrown out to him, and the efforts of his mother and sisters to matchmake. But then he had found Ariel and knew he wished to spend his life with her at his side. She had helped him to believe again in the goodness possible in this world, and to believe in himself. She had seen past his defenses, past his masquerade, and loved him anyway.

Now the last words were spoken, the ceremony was over, and friends and family surrounded them. Neither Ariel nor William could pretend to the cool aloofness so fashionable at weddings these days. No, they stayed side by side, hand in hand, as they hoped to do all their lives.

"How soon can we leave?" William whispered to his bride.

Ariel smiled up at him. "Impatient?" she asked.

Something flared in his eyes and found an answer in hers. "Very," he said, his voice husky.

"We could tell them our ship sails soon and we must be aboard," Ariel suggested, her own voice not entirely steady.

William grinned in reply. "So we could," he agreed, "if they did not know it sails tomorrow."

But there was no need for any such excuses. As Mrs. Merriweather said, quite firmly, a short time later, "You don't need all of us crowding you about when the two of you wish to be alone. Off with you! Go to wherever you are to stay tonight and have a wonderful trip. I envy you!"

"Do you wish you were off on such a trip?" the colonel asked, coming to stand with his arm around Mrs. Merriweather's waist.

She leaned against him. "Perhaps. Someday."

"Then, someday we shall go," Colonel Merriweather promised. "But now it is time to see these two young people off into their carriage."

Once Ariel and Stanfield were gone, Mrs. Merriweather continued to lean against her husband. "Who would have guessed, Andrew," she said, "that coming to London to sort out artifacts at the museum could possibly have such an outcome as this? What an adventure!"

But it was a mistake to remind the colonel. He immediately turned her to look at him. There was a frown on his face and a stern note to his voice as he said, "I do not like it, Marian! I do not like it at all, this penchant of yours for getting into difficult and dangerous situations. It has got to stop! Do you hear me? It has got to stop!"

Marian smiled, and in a soothing voice she said, "Yes, dear. Of course it does."

He grumbled, not entirely satisfied. "Never again, my dear! Is that quite clear?"

"Absolutely," Marian replied.

And then, before Colonel Merriweather could say another word, she kissed him. Just as, in the carriage, not so very far away, William was kissing Ariel. And a very pleasant distraction it was, for all of them.

# *Author's Note*

Mr. Hawthorne and Mr. Gilmer, indeed all the events in this story, are purely my imagination. So far as I know, no curator of the British Museum, or any person who worked there, has ever been involved in stealing and selling, or even "loaning" in this way, artifacts from the museum.

The British Museum was originally in Montagu House (sometimes spelled Montague House). There really were stuffed giraffes at the top of the main staircase. Until 1808, access to the museum was extremely limited, by ticket and only after one's credentials had been approved. By 1823, it was evident that a larger space was needed and work began on the new buildings. In 1842 Montagu House was demolished. But I had a great deal of fun imagining how things might have been in the Regency period!

Look for news of upcoming books at my Web site: http://www.sff.net/people/april.kihlstrom.

I love to hear from readers. I can be reached by e-mail at april.kihlstrom@sff.net.